HUMAN

COVEN: BOOK 13

DAVID NETH

DN Publishing

Human

Coven, Book 13

Batavia, NY

www.DavidNethBooks.com

ISBN: 978-1-963602-27-2
First Edition

Subscribe to the author's newsletter for updates and exclusive content:
DavidNethBooks.com/Newsletter

Follow the author at:
www.facebook.com/DavidNethBooks
www.instagram.com/dnpublishing

Also by David Neth

Lost By Magic
Lost By Magic
Lucky By Magic
Lured By Magic

Coven
Harpy
Siren
Valkyrie
Shapeshifter
Sorcerer
Witch (Short Story)
Enchantress
Oracle
Trickster
Poltergeist
Hex (Short Story)
Witch Hunter
Demon (Short Story)
Necromancer
Psychic (Short Story)
Incubus
Spirit (Short Story)
Human
Krampus (Short Story)
The Fates

Under the Moon
The Full Moon
The Harvest Moon
The Blood Moon
The Crescent Moon
The Blue Moon

The Art of Magic

Under the Moon: Villains
Toxanna (Short Story)
The Queen (Short Story)
The Dark Knight (Short Story)

Fuse
Origin
Omertá
Oblivion

Heat
Black Magnet
Dust Storm
The Gatekeeper

Standalone
All I Ever Wanted

CHAPTER 1

- OCTOBER 1990 -

As the rain hit the metal roof of the cabin, the sound ricocheted, bringing with it a peaceful white noise that seemed to cap the perfect day. The Williamsons had enjoyed a day of hiking, and had even cooked their lunch on a campfire just outside the cabin. It had been a warm fall day, which they were happy to spend as a family over the long weekend. Just one more night and then they'd be home and ready to jump back into their weekly routines.

With night quickly enveloping the sky, Lynn fussed with the propane stove at the small kitchenette inside the cabin. It had been heating just fine a minute ago, but now it seemed like everything was cooling off.

Her eight-year-old daughter, Crystal, lay on the couch near

the dying fire. Lynn watched as she tried to read her book in the dim light. The lightbulbs around the room didn't cast very much light throughout the cabin.

"Honey, can you even see the words on the pages?"

Crystal squinted. "Not really. And it's getting colder."

Lynn turned to her husband, who sat at the table beside the fire reading the newspaper.

"Larry, why don't you go out and get some firewood to restock the fire?" she suggested. "We don't want the temperature to drop too low in here overnight. It's supposed to dip down into freezing tonight. Oh, and see if you can spot a propane tank out on the porch or something. I think this one's out of juice."

"I didn't see an extra one."

She sighed and put one hand on her hip while the other poked at their dinner on the small skillet. "Can you please go check? Unless you'd rather eat half-cooked burgers for dinner."

He sighed heavily as he closed the newspaper with a loud crinkle. "I suppose, dear." He stood and reached his arms upward in a stretch. He held it for a few seconds before proceeding across the room and to the door.

They were all tired from hiking, and they were starting to snap at each other. That's why Lynn wanted to get everyone fed and keep them warm to prevent anymore snipes caused by hunger or discomfort. Herself included. They had had such a perfect weekend that she'd hate to see it ruined on their last night.

The cold air filled the room as Larry opened the door. The outer screen door slapped against the wood frame in his departure. There was a part of Lynn that loved that sound. As a kid, her parents would take her and her brother camping like this all the time. They often went in the summer time, but Lynn particularly loved those fall trips with the morning dew, the smell of the leaves, and the chill in the air.

Now that Lynn had a family of her own, she was insistent that those camping trips continue. And for the most part, Larry and Crystal loved the trips just as much.

The door swung open again and Larry quickly came inside. The screen door slapped against the frame again behind him. Softer this time, since Larry had closed the inner door so quickly and pressed his back against it.

"What's the matter?" Lynn saw the look of concern in her husband's eyes. Adding to that was his empty hands. Why hadn't he grabbed the wood that had been sitting just outside the door on the porch?

Larry locked the door. "Turn out the lights! Get down beneath the windows!"

Crystal sat up in the couch and looked at her father, then to her mother for reassurance. Panic was stricken across her face.

Lynn was annoyed at her husband for scaring their daughter, although by the look in her husband's face, she was starting to believe that he was serious. "Larry, what's—"

"Get down!"

Wordlessly, Lynn crossed the room to her daughter and led her to the front windows, where they lowered themselves down beneath the sill.

Larry peered through the window at the top of the door, then slunk down beside his family. "You didn't turn off the light!"

"You never told me what's going on," she countered.

Crystal brought her knees to her chest. "Mommy, what's going on?"

Lynn wrapped her arm tighter around her daughter. "I don't know, baby. It'll okay, though. It'll all be—"

"Shh!" Larry put a finger behind his ear, then whispered, "You hear that?"

Lynn's stomach dropped. She certainly did hear it. Voices. Men's voices. Just outside their windows.

Crystal huddled closer to her mother, quietly whimpering.

"It's okay. We'll all be okay." Lynn knew that nobody was buying her words—not even herself—but, as a mother, she felt them instinctively flow out of her.

The voices faded. The three of them sat in the growing darkness in silence. Even the single lightbulb hanging from the ceiling was flickering, as if it was about to go out.

Lynn made eye contact with her husband and mouthed: *Are they gone?*

Larry turned and peered out the window. Just a smidgen

at first, then he sat up straighter, allowing himself in full view of the window.

"You're scaring your daughter," Lynn said. The annoyance came from her hunger. Although her own fear was probably a factor too.

Larry fell back onto the floor and rested against the wall. He patted Crystal's leg. "I'm sorry, sweetie. It's okay. I just thought—well, it doesn't matter anymore. I was just overreacting."

"So there's no one outside?" Crystal asked.

Larry smiled. "No, sweetie. There's nothing to worry—"

The glass above them shattered as something came hurtling through the window. Moments later, white smoke quickly filled the room.

Crystal let out an ear-piercing scream.

CHAPTER 2

Samantha groaned. "I'm not sure I'm up for a camping trip. The cold, the damp air, sleeping the ground, none of it sounds appealing."

Kathy held the steering wheel loosely as she drove into the Allegheny National Forest. "It's only for a few days."

"Yeah, which is the longest I've ever gone away from Josh."

"Sam, we need this weekend to be just the two of us as sisters. Ever since I moved back in, we've done nothing but bicker with each other."

Samantha shrugged and looked out the window at the pine trees passing by them. "That's true. But with the rain we've been having and the temperature dropping, I'm not sure I'm really in the mood to camp."

"I'm *never* in the mood to camp," Kathy said. "Trust me. I hate it. This girl needs a warm, soft bed to sleep in each night and a hot shower to greet her in the morning. But judging from the flyer I picked up at the Chamber of Commerce, this place looks more like…remote living than traditional camping."

"*Remote living*?" Samantha asked.

"It has most of the comforts of home, but in a remote location."

"Hot water?"

"Got it."

"Electricity?"

"That too."

"Beds?"

"Twin size bunk beds, but they seemed to be nice and plump from the pictures. *And*, they have a fireplace, so that'll be nice."

Samantha couldn't deny that. She loved her fireplace back home and wished that there was one up in her and Steven's bedroom. But by the time the second story was added, technological advances didn't require a fireplace in each room. "Okay, what about a kitchen?"

"It's a kitchenette, but it has a stove burner, a sink, and a small fridge," Kathy said. "Everything we need, just…smaller."

"I hope you're right about this place." Samantha had been so busy at work and with Josh that she hadn't really been involved in the plans for this little girls' trip that Kathy had insisted on.

Of course, a part of her just didn't want to go on it at all, so subconsciously she had been avoiding planning it hoping that it would never come. Alas, that method had failed.

"Sam, we're going to have a good time," Kathy said. "We'll relax. Unwind. Talk. Play some cards. It'll be fun. It's been a while since it's been just the two of us."

"I know. It will be fun. But I'm a mother now, I can't *not* think about my kid."

"I get that, but I want you to focus on what we're going to do on this trip," Kathy countered. "Hiking, relaxing by the fire, listening to the wind blow the leaves, reading. You'll come back from this trip a whole new person."

"But I already miss him."

"I know, but he's in good hands. Steven is his father. He is more than capable of taking care of Josh. Plus, it's not like Josh is a tiny infant anymore. He's ten months old!"

It was hard to believe that Samantha's little baby boy was already past several of his first milestones and was quickly growing into a little toddler. It seemed like she had just been in the hospital giving birth. But then, she figured she'd probably be thinking that for the rest of his life. She felt as if she couldn't squeeze him enough, hold him enough, love him enough. And the thought of spending more time away from him than she had to was heart-wrenching.

"There's a turn up here, but I don't remember which one to take." Kathy squinted as she looked for the road signs along the curving road. "Check the map."

From the floor in front of her, Samantha pulled up the map and spread it out in her lap. "What road are we on now?"

"Route 666."

Samantha raised her eyebrows as she studied the map. "That seems like a bad sign."

"Oh, come on. It's just a route number. Stop trying to ruin this weekend already and just enjoy it. We just past Pierson Hill Road. I'm looking for Bobb's Creek Road. I know it's on the left, but how far up is it?"

"Um…not much farther, I don't think."

"How much is 'not much farther'?"

"Uh…I don't know. I think I lost track of where we are." Samantha turned the map, but none of it was making any sense. It didn't help that there were very few landmarks and so many twists and turns in the road.

"Here's a gas station," Kathy said. "I'll fill up and you go in and ask for directions." She pulled off the road to a single-pump station. An attendant stood out by the pump to fill up the car.

Once the car stopped, Samantha got out and walked to the tiny convenience store. Taped to the glass door were several missing persons postings. One for a man named Rick Gallagher and the other for Clay Clark. Both postings had pictures of men who were only about five or so years older than Samantha and Kathy themselves.

Samantha shook her head. It was a shame when any two

people, but especially two *young* people just up and disappeared. But what stood out to her was that they were both men. And, judging by the looks of them, they were men who looked like they could take care of themselves. The fact that they had gone missing spoke of something else.

But Samantha didn't want to think about that.

She opened the door and tried to put it out of her mind, but she couldn't help but feel the sense of dread that something terrible was coming. There were so many signs: Route 666, the missing persons, Samantha's unease with the trip from the very beginning.

Then again, she and Kathy had faced worse things than anything that could possibly be lurking in the woods. What she was feeling was probably a mixture of parent guilt and sister guilt. Being trapped between a rock and a hard place. She couldn't spend all her time with her son and ignore her sister. And she couldn't spend alone time with her sister without being away from her son.

"Can I help you?" the store clerk asked when she walked up to the counter. He was a late-middle-aged man with salt-and-pepper hair and a completely gray mustache. He wore a flannel shirt and jeans. Wedged between two of his fingers, a cigarette burned in his hand.

"Hi, my sister and I are camping out here and we got turned around," Samantha said. "Would you be able to help point me in the right direction?"

The man took a puff of his cigarette, then smiled and let the smoke slip out of his mouth. "Sure thing, madam! Lay that map right here and let's see if we can't get you to where you're looking to go."

Samantha set the map down and pointed to a particular route running through the forest. "We're here, right?"

"No, ma'am." He pointed to another spot further down on the same route. "We're all the way down here. Where is it you're heading to?"

"Shady Acres."

The man sat back, surprise on his face. "The Fisher property?"

Samantha pulled out the flyer from her back pocket. Sure enough, on the back it said that Shady Acres was owned by the Fisher family. "I guess so."

"Are you sure you want to go there?" He raised his eyebrows as he looked at her.

"Uh…well…" Samantha hesitated, her fears about this weekend on high alert. "I mean, we've already paid for a cabin, so yes, we do."

He took another puff of his cigarette and nodded slowly. "Okay then. Just be careful out there. Now, here's what you need to do. Keep going down this route, then you'll want to turn left onto Bobb's Creek Road. It's hidden in the trees. Dirt road, drive slow, make sure you put it in low gear because the inclines out here can be murder on your engine. Now, the Fisher property will be on your right once you turn onto Bobb's Creek. It's at the top of a hill. The driveway's hidden. Not many people go down there, so you'll have to keep your eyes open for it."

Samantha nodded. "Got it. Thanks."

"You said it was you and your sister who were staying there?"

"Yeah."

"You don't have any boyfriends or anyone else staying with you?"

"My husband's back at home with our son." She felt her heart rate begin to pick up. "Why?"

He shrugged and averted his eyes. "Just curious. Be careful out there."

Samantha forced a smile. "Thanks for the tip—and the directions. I appreciate it."

She turned and left the convenience store, trying her best not to worry about the encounter she had just had.

"Ready?" Kathy asked back at the car.

"Yep." As Samantha climbed back in, she considered telling Kathy about her conversation with the helpful store clerk—or the missing persons postings—but she didn't. As the older sibling, and the one who was already having reservations about this trip, she decided to take on the burden of worry all on her own.

Using the directions Samantha had been given, they found their way to Shady Acres without a problem. The tip the clerk had offered about low gear helped Kathy navigate the car up the steep incline on the gravel road without the tires spinning out or the engine overexerting itself.

"He said it would be hidden," Samantha said as she studied the passing greenery for any signs or break in the overgrowth. "There!"

Kathy hit the brakes—perhaps harder than she needed to—and pivoted the car down a gravel driveway. Branches scraped the side of the car as they passed through a particularly tight spot in the brush before opening up to a clearing with a wide driveway where there were two trucks parked. To the right side of the driveway was a two-story barn and to the left was a ramshackle house.

Based on the crude map on the back of the flyer from the Chamber of Commerce, that was the "main house." Samantha had envisioned something more regal or stately. Instead, the house looked tired. Paint had chipped off the siding, other spots had dry rotted wood, and the roof looked a little worse for wear. Beside it sat several rusted cars in the weeds. Over the hum of the engine, they heard dogs barking from somewhere that Samantha couldn't place.

But through the front door on the porch, the warm glow of light came through and the house looked warm and inviting inside. Maybe, Samantha figured, she shouldn't judge a book by its cover.

"*This* is it?" Kathy asked, looking at the house.

"Yeah." Samantha pointed to the sign at the front of the driveway that said "Shady Acres." It looked identical to the one on the flyer. "And over there is probably where the road to the cabins are." She pointed to the driveway that passed right by the barn. It was filled with muddy potholes, but was very clearly meant for vehicles.

"Oh. The trees over there look nice with the colors," Kathy said. "Maybe the cabins are really nice too."

Samantha reached for her sister's arm before she could exit. "Are you sure you want to stay here? We could change our minds. It was only a two-hour drive."

"Yes, I'm sure. And I'm exhausted from the drive. Plus, we've already paid, so let's just go check it out." Kathy pulled her arm free from her sister's grasp, but paused before opening the door, her eyes locked on the house. "It does look kind of creepy, though, doesn't it?"

Samantha nodded.

"We're just being paranoid. We'll be fine." Kathy looked back at Samantha and smiled. "Besides, we're witches. They can't hold a candle to us."

"Famous last words," Samantha grumbled as she climbed out of the car as well.

The two sisters walked up to the front porch, neither of them having a good feeling about their lodgings.

CHAPTER 3

- 1980 -

Even from his room at the end of his family's trailer, fifteen-year-old Donovan Fisher could hear his parents arguing. It was always the same things that spawned the arguments: suspected infidelity, insecurities, laziness. Their constant arguing was why Donovan had decided that he was never getting married. It just seemed like a waste. Two people who lived together, relied on each other to survive, but couldn't stand each other?

No, Donovan would learn how to be self-sufficient so he wouldn't ever have to rely on anyone else.

Of course, his parents weren't the only example of a married couple that Donovan was exposed to. There was also his Uncle Jim and Aunt Sue, who owned the property

Donovan and his parents lived on.

Uncle Jim and Aunt Sue seemed like a solid couple. *That* was the type of marriage Donovan could see having someday. But how often did a good marriage like theirs happen? Uncle Jim and Aunt Sue's marriage worked because both were self-sufficient. At least, Uncle Jim was. He owned his land, hunted his land, and rented out even more land closer to the city for farmers to farm on. He provided for his family without ever having to leave home. Meanwhile, Aunt Sue stayed back at the house, cooked up the food that was farmed on their land, and kept up with everything else on the homestead. They were a team.

"You're always eyeing her up!" Donovan's mother, Gretchen, shouted across the small trailer. "Every time we go in there, you're suddenly all softy and, 'Oh, is there anything I can help you with to make your shift a little easier?'" Donovan heard a gagging sound and then, "It's *disgusting*! And embarrassing. I seen the way you been looking at her!"

"I ain't looking at no one!" Rodney, Donovan's father, shouted back. "Besides, is it a crime to offer a little help? It's not like I'm pressing myself up against her and playing dumb like you do to them guys at the bar!"

"It's called flirting for bigger tips, Rod! If I didn't do that, we wouldn't be able to afford this piece of shit we live in! Don't think your whore at the gas station can afford nothing more than this!"

"There's nothing going on! Would you drop it?"

"No, because I know you been lying through them teeth! You come up with every excuse in the book to go see her! Are you screwing her? Tell me, so I know whether I'm going to catch any diseases from that slut."

"Can't catch nothing when we ain't sleeping together!"

Donovan had heard enough. He wanted out, but the only way out was through the only door in the trailer. If he made a quick exit while they were arguing, maybe they wouldn't even notice.

He opened the door and paused to see what kind of reaction he'd get from his parents. When they paid him no mind, he walked quickly to the door, but as he put his hand on the handle, his mother's voice rose.

"And where the hell do you think *you're* going, Don?"

He turned and kept one hand on the doorknob. "Going over to Uncle Jim's for a bit."

"Oh." Her tone softened a little. "Well, don't stay over there too long. I want to see you before I head off to work."

Rodney snorted. "Yeah. Your mother needs to get all gussied up so some stranger can put his hands on her."

"I told you, that's for *tips*!"

"If that was true, we wouldn't be living on my brother's property."

"That's because you can't get off your ass and find a—"

Donovan made his escape while they were distracted. Once

outside, he went right behind the trailer and into the thick of the woods.

Uncle Jim said he liked to keep his property in the Allegheny Mountains as natural as possible to encourage the wildlife to settle there so they could hunt and provide for the family. So there was no set trail, other than the ones the deer had made themselves.

As far back as Donovan could remember, Uncle Jim had always been bringing them extra venison or turkey meat that he got while hunting. He loved hunting and had even begun teaching Donovan how to do it properly. Everything from what to wear, what to look for, and what different animals were attracted to, to preparing the meat for eating and how to cook it for best the best taste. Uncle Jim knew everything and Donovan was like a sponge, absorbing it all eagerly.

By the time Donovan reached Uncle Jim's house, he saw his cousins, Pete and Kurt, out back with Uncle Jim target-practicing with their rifles. Donovan's shoulders sunk a little at the sight, but still he went up to greet them.

Donovan didn't have his own gun. Sure, Uncle Jim let him borrow his whenever, but he didn't have his own to practice at home. And the one time he had asked his parents for one, Donovan's father laughed in his face and told him how they could barely afford food and cigarettes, so why in the hell would they buy him a gun?

"Mind if I jump in?" Donovan asked his cousins in

greeting. "When you're done."

Pete and Kurt both nodded at him, then returned to aiming their rifles.

Donovan sat on a nearby stack of pallets and swung his feet under him, trying not to look too pathetic. Sure, this was better than listening to his parents argue, but he still didn't quite feel like he fit in.

"Donovan!" Uncle Jim's voice boomed across the yard.

He turned and saw his uncle waving him toward the barn. He jumped down and hurried across the yard to join his uncle.

"How you been, son?"

"I'm okay," Donovan said. "Mom and Dad are fighting again, so I thought I'd come over here."

Uncle Jim let out a heavy sigh, then reached for a rifle from his work bench. It was a new one, Donovan recognized that much. He had a slight fascination with firearms. Perhaps because he wasn't allowed to own one. Or maybe it was because Uncle Jim and Pete and Kurt all had one of their own.

"I have a surprise for you," Uncle Jim said. "But you can't tell your parents about it—especially your father. Understand? I don't want him to feel emasculated or nothing."

Donovan nodded. He wasn't *quite* sure what *emasculated* meant, but he knew it was bad.

"Here's your very own .22."

Donovan hesitantly reached for it with wide eyes. "Seriously?"

Uncle Jim smiled. "You've earned it, son. Now get out there and target practice along with your cousins. You're going to need it."

CHAPTER 4

"Why, hello!" Although she wore a smile, the woman who answered the door was very plain. Her hair hung limply around her round face, most of it having fallen out of the clip she had used to keep it back out of her face. Her dress looked worn, having likely once boasted a vibrant floral pattern but now looked tired and limp. She wore an apron, which was discolored with stains from sauces, olive oil, and other messy items from the kitchen. "You must be our newest guests." She held out a hand, first to Samantha, then Kathy. "I'm Sue Fisher."

"I'm Samantha Harper, and this is my sister, Kathy Walker," Samantha said. "I believe my sister booked one of your cabins over the phone?"

Sue smiled at Kathy. "Yes, I have your paperwork all ready. Come on in. Have a seat at the dining room table."

The sisters followed her in and stepped right into the dining room. The table took up most of the room and the end of it was covered with sweaters, flannels, and hats—all of which gave off an odor of sweat and were dirtied with mud. There were some boots lined by the door and camouflaged overalls hanging over the back of the chair at the other end of the table.

"Could I get either of you any tea or coffee? Or anything else to drink? We have water, iced tea, and lemonade. Oh, and I believe I have some apple cider down in the cellar if you'd rather that."

Kathy smiled politely. "No, thank you. We're just anxious to get settled into our cabin."

Sue nodded with a tight smile. "Okay, dear. Let me grab your paperwork and I'll let my husband, Jim, know that you're here."

When she left, the sisters exchanged nervous glances, but neither of them shared any words in the quiet environment. Samantha took the opportunity to look at the pictures that lined the walls. Family photos, young and old. Grandparents holding newborns, parents pushing children on swings, adult siblings standing stoically beside one another.

Family.

Samantha sat back in her chair. Maybe there was nothing to worry about. This was a home. The feelings she'd been having was nothing but paranoia and sadness over leaving Josh for the weekend. The Fishers weren't dangerous.

Heavy boots sounded on the hardwood, which carried a tall, imposing man in through the doorway. He wore a plaid flannel shirt over his wide shoulders that was tucked into his jeans.

"Good afternoon, ladies," he said in a deep, husky voice. "I'm Jim Fisher. I believe you've already met my wife."

Samantha nodded. "We did. I'm Samantha and this is my sister, Kathy. We're here to check into one of your cabins."

"Here's their paperwork, dear." Sue appeared from around the corner and passed Jim a file folder.

"Thanks, honey." He took a seat, then looked back at his wife. "Could you run down to the cellar and get me something to drink?"

"Of course. I'll be right up."

After she left, Jim turned to the sisters and pulled out the papers from the folder. "The rules are pretty simple. No defacing or altering the property in any way, no open flames in the cabin—outside of the fireplace—your trash needs to be put in the dumpster on your way out at the end of your stay. If you have any food, that needs to be locked up every night." His eyes bore into them. "Be very careful with that. We have bears out here looking for food, and they're not shy about it. Unfortunately, we've had a few unfortunate circumstances because of recklessness. Don't let that be you."

Samantha stiffened at his words, which struck her as more of a challenge than a warning. "Don't worry about us. We'll be careful."

He smirked. "I'm sure you will. But I wouldn't feel right if I didn't warn you."

Samantha considered using her telepathic abilities to read his mind, but she held back. That would be an abuse of power. She couldn't go around head-hopping everyone who made her mad. Everyone had a right to their own private thoughts.

"My boys and I have been working on creating hiking trails throughout the property, even linking one of them up to one of the state trails that runs through the National Forest, which surrounds our property. These trails are still a work in progress, but I've taken the liberty of creating this map for your enjoyment." Across the table he passed a copy of a hand-drawn map. "It's not perfect, and it's not to scale, but it'll help tell you which trails connect to each other."

Kathy took it and peered it over. It looked like it had been hand-drawn and photocopied. "How many miles are these trails?"

"We haven't measured it specifically, but I'm guessing close to fifty, maybe more. Make sure you take the map with you when you go hiking. Wouldn't want you to get lost in the woods. And be careful of the terrain. It gets quite steep in some places. We've tried to level things out where we can, but we tried to preserve the natural landscape as well."

"We'll stick to the easy trails then," Samantha said.

Jim smirked. "Not sure if any of these could be considered *easy*, but I'll let you figure that out for yourself. If you need anything, don't hesitate to stop back up here at the main house. If I'm not available, either one of my boys could help you, or my nephew. Taking care of our guests is our favorite thing to do."

Again, Samantha couldn't quite read his tone, but sensed an undying meaning behind it. She and Jim studied each other across the table for several long seconds.

Finally, he broke the tense moment by pulling out another piece of paper and sliding it to Samantha. "This is your standard agreement, stating that you understand the rules and agree to adhere to them. I need you both to sign it."

Samantha skimmed the document and saw that it was, indeed, a standard agreement, similar to what guests needed to sign when they checked into a hotel. She grabbed the pen in front of her and signed it before passing it to Kathy to do the same.

When both of their signatures had been added, Jim collected the paperwork back in the folder, then set a key on the table in front of the girls.

"You ladies will be staying in Cabin 8, out toward the back of the property." He raised his hand to indicate just how far it was. "It's the best one we have, down near the creek, surrounded by trees. It's the closest to the middle of nowhere you'll ever be."

Samantha doubted that, considering the places that she and

her sister had been in their lives, but she let it pass.

"Just follow the road past the barn. There'll be signs directing you which way to go."

Kathy reached for the key. "All right. Is there anything else you need from us?"

"No, ma'am." He sat back in his chair. "I hope you ladies enjoy your stay."

"Thank you for everything." Samantha quickly led her sister out of the house and back to the car.

The thought of spending another second under his imposing glare was too much for her. She only hoped the cabin was more friendly.

CHAPTER 5

Samantha squinted as she peered out the window, trying to read the signs from far away. She swore her eyes were getting worse with age, but she refused to go see an eye doctor.

Besides, she could make out the homemade signs along the side of the narrow road if she only squinted her eyes a little.

"These damn potholes," Kathy murmured as the car jerked over another one. The contents of the car shook and another bag clunked against the back door. "Any idea how much further?"

"No idea," Samantha said. "It can't be that far, though. They can't own *that* much property. Especially not if they need to maintain all of these cabins."

They had been driving for nearly ten minutes since leaving

the Fisher house. They had passed two roads, the first one leading to Cabins 1-3, and the second leading to Cabins 4-6. Shortly after that they had passed Cabin 7, which left Cabin 8.

"Well, what do the signs say?" Kathy slowed the car as she guided it over another large hole. "I'm not really paying attention with how terrible this road is. You'd think they'd fill in these holes if they expect their guests to travel them."

"Maybe they're pouring all their money into the cabins."

"I hope."

"The signs just say that Cabin 8 is this way—WATCH OUT!"

Kathy slammed on the brakes as a deer came darting out of the brush. At the sight of the car, the deer immediately darted back out of sight.

The girls sat still as their hearts slowed back to their normal rates.

"Holy hell that scared the shit out of me," Samantha said.

"Me too. Welcome to the woods, I guess."

Of course, they had seen deer on their way into the mountains, but the overgrowth hadn't been as thick along the main road as it was this deep in the Fisher property.

Samantha put her hand to her chest to try to even out her breathing. "Okay. We're overreacting. We need to calm down."

Kathy eased the car forward, keeping an eye out for more deer. "That'd be easier to do if we weren't staying in Murderville, USA."

"You picked it out."

"Don't remind me. Do you think it'd be rude if we turned around and checked out already?"

Samantha looked across the car at her sister. "Um…yes, that would be very rude. Not to mention, if we really *are* staying in Murderville, as you put it, then checking out early would only piss off the murderers."

"Damn. I hate it when you're right."

Samantha took a deep breath. "Jim and Sue just seem a little…rustic. There's nothing bad about being a little rough around the edges. And just think, in two days we'll be on our way home. Even then, we won't really have to see the Fishers all weekend. Not if our cabin is at the back of the property like this. We can do our own thing and then check out on the way back home."

Truthfully, she was trying to convince herself that everything would be all right just as much as she was trying to convince Kathy. She thought of Josh and hoped that he was happy and content at home. She knew Steven was taking good care of him, but she missed seeing how happy her son was with her own eyes. This was going to be a long weekend.

Kathy leaned back against the seat with both hands on the wheel. She let out a heavy sigh. "You're right. I'm just nervous about how this cabin is going to look, but the pictures from the flyer looked okay."

The road began to point downward at a steep angle.

"Shift into low gear," Samantha warned. She held onto the handle above the door and braced against the back of Kathy's seat with her other hand. "And easy on the brakes."

Kathy struggled to keep control of the wheel as she eased the car down the bumpy slope. "It's hard to go easy on them when the road still has potholes and washouts."

"You'd think they would've fixed this," Samantha said.

"The rain probably washed it all out."

The road finally leveled out again and Kathy steered the car into a grassy clearing. There were a few mature trees sprinkled throughout the lawn, giving a comfortable definition between shade and sunshine. Leaves covered the ground, and the ones that remained in the tree were shades of vibrant oranges, reds, and yellows. At the edge of the clearing near a rocky creek, Cabin 8 sat facing the direction of the water.

"Oh, this is pretty." Samantha looked around.

"We'll be lucky if nothing broke off the car on that way down," Kathy said. "And the way out of here is going to be brutal. Can you imagine trying to go *up* that hill?"

"We'll manage." Samantha pointed. "Looks like there's a little parking area next to the cabin.

Kathy maneuvered the car to the small spot beside the cabin and turned off the car. She let out a breath of air. "Feels good to be done traveling for today."

"We still need to unpack."

"Should we check out the cabin first? I'm dying to see what

it looks like." Kathy tried to scope it out through the windshield, but she couldn't see much through the few windows in the cabin.

"Sure."

The entrance was from the front of the cabin, which was directed at the creek. Clearly, this cabin was built for pure relaxation. Anyone staying here was encouraged to shut out the rest of the world. Samantha liked the idea of stepping out onto the porch in the morning, enjoying her coffee while watching the leaves fall and listening to the water rush over the rocks.

"Look, Sam, there's a fire pit by the creek," Kathy said. "If we can find some firewood, we should have a fire out here one of these nights."

Samantha stepped onto the porch and saw a stack by the door. "Here's some. Must be for the fireplace inside, but I'm sure we could also use it for the fire pit."

"Okay, I'm warming up to the idea of this cabin," Kathy admitted. "Sounds nice so far."

"Let's hope the inside is just as nice." Samantha unlocked the door and stepped inside.

"It's small."

"Sure, it's small. It's a cabin."

Kathy brushed past her sister to step further inside. Inside was all one room, except for one small room. "Here's the bathroom. Seems clean enough."

"Kitchenette doesn't look bad," Samantha said from around the corner.

Kathy stopped behind the couch in front of the fireplace. "Found the issue: bunk beds." There were two sets of bunk beds built into the wall, which allowed for a total of four people to share one cabin.

"Didn't you see that in the flyer?"

She sighed. "Yeah. I just hoped that part would be different."

Samantha smiled, feeling better about their home away from home. "It's clean. And cozy. Plus, neither of us needs to climb up onto the top bunk."

"Yeah, I guess you're right."

The sisters were quiet as they looked around. Both of them tried to dispel any reservations they had about their stay. Something still nagged at Samantha, but she tried not to pay it any mind.

"All right," Kathy said. "Let's go unpack the car."

CHAPTER 6

Kathy woke up the next morning to the sound of clicking. For a moment, she forgot where she was. Then, as she stretched out and her hand hit the wooden railing preventing her from falling off the bed, she remembered—they were in Cabin 8 and Kathy was in one of the bunks flanking the fireplace.

She sat up and narrowly missed smacking her head on the top bunk. She rubbed her eyes, pulling her messy hair into a bun. Across the room, Samantha was at the propane skillet with a lighter pointed at the burner while she tried to get it to light.

"Having trouble?" Kathy asked in a groggy voice.

"I'm getting it." A second later, the burners *whooshed* to life and Samantha smiled. "Aha! See? Just what I intended."

Kathy climbed out of bed and joined her sister in the kitchenette. "Need any help with breakfast?"

"There's not really anything you can help with." Samantha placed the few sausages they had brought from home on the skillet, then cracked several eggs and added them beside the frying meat.

"Looks like it's going to be a nice day." Kathy perched herself at the small table near the back window, where she had a nice view of the creek. Not as nice as the front porch, but still an enjoyable view. "The sun is already shining and I don't think they're calling for rain at all this weekend. Should be a good day to hike."

"Let's hope." Samantha set a couple of paper plates beside the skillet, and began looking around for the plastic cutlery they had packed. "All I know is that you're going to have to temper your pace for me because other than evening walks pushing a stroller, I haven't done any strenuous activity since Josh was born."

"Sam, you need to give yourself more credit than that," Kathy said. "You look great and you're in better shape than you realize. Not to mention, this weekend is about you and me spending time together, not about exercise. That's just a secondary benefit."

"Yeah, well, we'll see about that." Samantha flipped the sausages. "The food will be ready in just a few minutes."

"You know what? I think I forgot my hiking boots at home."

"What did you bring?"

"Just an old pair of sneakers, which I thought I'd wear *after* our big day of hiking." Kathy made a face. "Shoot."

"Aren't those boots on the front porch yours?"

"What boots?"

"The ones on the porch." Samantha stepped away from the skillet long enough to point the spatula out the window by the porch.

Kathy followed and peered through the window herself. "No, those aren't mine." She opened the front door and stepped into the chilly morning air. The wooden porch floor felt cold on her feet, so she tiptoed quickly to retrieve the boots and bring them back into the warmth.

"If they're not yours, then why are you touching them?"

"They're not grimy or anything." Kathy retook her seat at the small table. "Actually, they're pretty nice. Why would someone leave them?" She stuck her hand inside to make sure there were no bugs or cobwebs. Everything felt intact. She slid one on her foot.

"Kathy! That's disgusting!"

"It fits!" the younger sister cheered. "Looks like I found my hiking boots!"

"You're really going to wear those all day?" Samantha was back at the skillet, setting their breakfast onto two paper plates she had set out.

Kathy slid on the second boot and began walking around

the cabin. "Sure. They feel great. Perfect fit, almost. And even if they weren't, it's better than my feet killing me all weekend from not wearing good support while we're hiking."

Samantha sighed. "Whatever you say. They're your feet." She set the paper plates on the small table. "The food's ready. Come and eat."

They ate in silence, both of them watching out the window at the water running through the creek and the leaves falling from the trees. It was relaxing. And Kathy was very excited to get outside and start exploring. She had never really been an outdoorsy person, but she was looking forward to the day ahead of them.

After breakfast, they each took showers, then loaded up a day bag filled with water bottles and snacks, then locked the cabin behind them, and headed out into the woods to begin the day's adventure.

CHAPTER 7

Samantha plopped down on a rock along the trail to catch her breath. She was doing okay, for the most part. And it didn't feel as though she was slowing Kathy down, which was a good thing. But they had climbed up a pretty steep incline and the rock was a perfect seat to take in the clearing of trees that allowed them to overlook the mountains.

Kathy sat beside her sister and pulled the day bag off of her back. "Wow, that's beautiful." She pulled out two water bottles and handed one to her sister before opening the other and taking a sip.

"It's such a perfect day," Samantha said. "You can see the colors of the leaves for miles." She took a long sip of her water and watched as the birds soared through the air before disappearing into the trees.

"Snack?" Kathy offered her a granola bar.

"Sure. But we need to make sure the wrappers come with us and end up in the trash. You heard what Jim Fisher said about bears around here."

"Yes, I did. But we haven't seen any signs of them."

"Would you even know what to look for?" Samantha asked. "How do you know we haven't seen any signs?"

Kathy shrugged. "I guess that's true." She looked down at something behind the rock Samantha was sitting on.

"What is it?" Samantha turned to try to see, but the angle wasn't working in her favor. Luckily, Kathy pulled whatever it was out of its hiding spot.

"It's a wallet." Kathy opened the black leather and found the driver's license in the plastic window. "It's for Larry Finkel." She turned to her older sister for recognition, but neither of them had heard the name before.

"He must've dropped it when he was hiking and never found it," Samantha suggested. "We probably should take it down to the main house and give it to the Fishers so they can get in touch with him and get it back to him."

Kathy groaned. "Can't we just leave it on their porch when we check out tomorrow?"

"And hope that it gets back to him? Kathy, the Fishers would have his contact information. For all we know, Larry is from across the country."

The younger sister put her finger in the air. "Um, actually they're from the Pittsburgh area. So not that far."

"But not exactly on our way home, either. I want to get home and see Josh tomorrow. I don't want to take a detour because the people who own this property are *creepy*. We've faced worse than that, Kathy."

Her shoulders slumped. "I know. I know. It's probably the best thing to do."

Samantha inspected the hand-drawn map Jim Fisher had given her. "If I'm reading this right, there's a fork in the trail up ahead. If we take the one on the left, we can loop back around and make our way to the main house. Then, depending on the time, we can just take the road back to our cabin."

Kathy was busy inspecting the other contents of the wallet. "Uh-huh."

"Would you put that away! That's the man's private business."

"Here's a picture of him." She held it out for Samantha to see.

There he was, a growing belly protruding farther than his chest, but otherwise well-kept. His wife stood beside him, as tall as him and thin. Her long blonde hair was pulled over one shoulder and her hand rested on the shoulder of her daughter, who hovered several inches shorter than her. The little girl was certainly the daughter of both husband and wife. She had the round face of her father, but the bright blonde hair of her mother.

"Cute family," Samantha said. "Even more reason not to hold off on getting it back to them."

"How long do you think this extra detour is going to take?"

"I don't know. The map isn't marked with distance. But, considering we have to go all the way back to the main house, I'd say it's going to take a couple hours. We'll probably be back at the cabin in time to make dinner."

Kathy let out a big breath of air. "Well, we wanted a hike. Better get moving, then, I guess." She stood, then offered her hand to help her sister up.

The trail back to the main house was less impressive than the one they had taken that morning. They were walking through the woods, and while there were several picture-perfect moments throughout, there weren't mountain views to see the changing colors like there had been on the stretch they had taken that morning. Not only that, but the fall weather brought in clouds that left them feeling a little chilly and fearing the possibility of rain.

They moved quickly along the trail, chatting idly about this and that until Samantha decided to focus more on her breathing to keep up with her sister than to maintain a conversation with her.

Finally, after a couple hours, they came up to a bend in the road that revealed the back of the main house. Oddly, the sight of it didn't bring a sense of relief to the girls at all.

"Are you sure we can't just mail it to him?" Kathy asked as they walked up to the front porch.

"And risk his wallet, his credit cards, and all of his cash getting lost in the mail? I don't think so."

Kathy swallowed her fear down as Samantha knocked on the door. Through the window, they could see lights on in the kitchen, and they could faintly hear the chatter of the television.

The door opened and a figure appeared in the doorway. He stood behind the screen door and with the light coming from behind him, the girls couldn't make out his face. Samantha knew for sure that it wasn't Jim, so it had to be one of his kids. She hadn't expected the kids to be so *grown*. But, judging by how old both Jim and Sue looked, she supposed she should've assumed that their children would be young adults themselves.

"Can I help you?"

"I hope so," Samantha said. "We're staying in one of your cabins. Is your father home?"

"My father's dead."

"Oh," was all Samantha could muster as a response. She wasn't expecting that and the coldness in his voice sent shivers down her spine.

Behind her, Samantha felt Kathy take a half step backward, while also tightening her hold on Samantha's arm.

The awkward silence between the three of them lingered until the man finally said, "But my uncle's home."

"And you are...?" Kathy asked.

"Donovan."

"Well, Donovan, can we speak to your uncle?" Samantha had read somewhere that using someone's name disarmed them. She didn't know if it was true, but she figured it couldn't hurt. "Or your aunt."

Donovan simply nodded, then closed the door behind him and disappeared back inside.

The sisters exchanged looks, both of them silently noting that he never invited them in, out of the cold darkening evening.

Inside the house, another shadowy figure appeared. This time, however, Samantha recognized him as Jim. He opened both doors and stepped out onto the porch. He crossed his arms, bracing against the chill.

"What can I help you girls with?" he asked.

"We were hiking through some of your trails and we found this." Samantha handed him the wallet.

Jim opened it and inspected the identification. "Hmm. He was a guest of ours just last week."

"He was?" Samantha asked, hope filling her voice.

"We were hoping you could get in touch with him to return it," Kathy added.

"Might be better off just mailing it to him, but I'll give him a call and see what he'd prefer me to do. Thank you for returning it to me."

"Of course," Samantha said with a smile. "We figured you'd

have his contact information somewhere."

Jim looked out across the driveway toward the barn. "It's getting late. You girls better hurry up back to your cabin. Or would you rather I gave you a lift?"

"No, that's okay," Kathy blurted.

Samantha smiled again, more forced this time. "We're trying to get our exercise in."

"Well, you'd better hurry up. Daylight dwindles fast this time of year and you don't want to be stuck out in these woods in the middle of the night." With that, he turned and went back inside, closing the door behind him.

Kathy waited until they were halfway across the driveway to say, "That seemed odd. The *whole family* seems odd. I'm just glad our cabin is as far away from them as possible."

Samantha shook her head and chanced one last look back at the house. In the window, she saw someone watching them. She swore it looked just like Donovan's shadow, but she couldn't be sure with the distance. Turning back to her sister, Samantha gripped Kathy's arm and quickened their pace down the road. "Jim is hiding something. They all are. I could sense it."

"Could you get a reading as to what it is?"

She shook her head again. "Not while I was talking, and nothing that I could decipher from all the lies and stories they had told over the years. But there's definitely something there. I want to stay as far away from them from now on as possible."

Kathy kept her eyes on the potholed road, careful not to

miss a step and twist her ankle. "Well, tomorrow will be the last time we ever have to talk to them. This is our last night here."

"Yeah." Samantha looked back again. The house was completely out of sight, but that sense of dread in the pit of her stomach was growing again. "I think we should pack up and leave first thing in the morning."

"We can pack up the car tonight with as much as we can," Kathy suggested.

"Good idea. The more we talk to those people, the more suspicious I am of them."

CHAPTER 8

- 1982 -

Donovan and Pete ran through the woods, cheering and hollering. The thrill of the hunt ran deep in their bones. For the boys, this was as close to natural as they could get. It was like returning to their ancestral roots of hunting and gathering. Only with modernized weapons.

The doe they were chasing down had been shot in the leg by Pete. Nothing life-threatening. And the instinct response of fight or flight kicked in for the animal, giving it adrenaline to run off. But the way that Pete shot it, both boys knew it wouldn't get very far before the leg gave out and she'd be a sitting duck.

Just like they suspected, the doe lay on its injured leg in a clearing in the woods. At the sight of the boys, she scratched at the ground to try to get back to her feet to run, but her hind leg was useless.

"Say goodnight!" Pete raised his rifle to fire, but Donovan held out his hand to his cousin.

"Wait!"

"What?"

"Isn't this a little...boring?"

"This isn't fun for you?" Pete lowered the gun.

"Sure it is, but couldn't it be *more* fun?"

"What do you mean?"

"I think we should play with it for a bit."

The two boys stared at each other. Their silence broken only by Kurt catching up to them with ragged breaths.

"Didn't you hear me calling for you to wait?" the younger brother asked. He hunched over and leaned on his knees to get his breath back. His rifle was slung over his shoulder.

"What did you have in mind?" Pete asked Donovan, ignoring his brother.

Donovan watched the struggling doe as he thought it over. "We could set a trap for it somewhere. Let it go. Make it think that it's free. Lure it into a trap and then—BAM! *That's* when we shoot it. Or something like that."

Pete made a face. "I don't know. I'd rather just shoot it." He turned in the direction of the doe and raised his gun again. "I mean, she's laying right here."

Donovan put his hand on the barrel of the gun and forced it

down. "Trust me. It's a doe. It's not going to fight back. Not like a buck would. We can play with this one."

"You mean torture," Kurt said from behind them.

"Torture sounds too cruel. Too dark." Donovan shrugged and smirked. "We're just going to have some fun. The damn thing is going to die anyway."

Both Pete and Kurt exchanged glances.

Donovan handed his rifle to Pete and approached the deer. It started clawing at the dirt in earnest. Donovan reached his hand down and gripped the thin, injured leg, and began to pull.

The deer flailed, kicking out with its good legs and finally making contact with Donovan's arm.

"Ow!" He jerked back. "The damn thing hit me!" He inspected his arm and saw that the hoof had seared through his jacket.

Pete rushed up and went at the doe with his boot. Kicking it first in the belly then, as the deer began to kick at him, he aimed for its legs, it's back, even its head. Anything that would deliver a good punishment without himself getting hit.

Only, he was getting hit. Just like the doe's hooves sliced through Donovan's jacket, it was doing the same to Pete's jeans. Blood soaked the denim.

"Pete, stop!" Kurt called from behind him. "You're bleeding! And you're bruising the meat! Dad's going to be pissed!"

The older brother didn't stop. He continued to swing his foot into the doe's belly.

The sound of gunfire rang out throughout the woods. Kurt held the rifle to where the deer's head had once been, now in pieces all over the leaves.

With heavy breaths, the three boys stared at one another. Something had changed in this hunt. Something that could never be reversed. They were all changed. Forever.

"Are you all right?" Pete asked Donovan.

He patted at his arm. "No blood. It just caught the sleeve. What about you? There's a good amount of blood on your jeans."

Pete looked down at his pants and moved his legs for a better view. "I'll be fine. They're just surface wounds. Scratches, really. The damn thing was too stupid to do any real damage."

"We should get the truck," Kurt said. "Start dragging the body out. Maybe there's still some good meat on it, even though Pete kicked the shit out of it."

"Mostly in its belly," Pete said. "We're going to take all those organs out anyway."

"I think it's a good idea to go back, though," Donovan agreed. "We promised your dad that we'd get meat to start stocking up the freezer for the winter. He's going to be pissed if we come back empty-handed."

Neither of his cousins responded. They were both staring at something beyond Donovan. He turned to see what they were looking at and saw Uncle Jim standing there, grinding his jaw.

He was already pissed.

CHAPTER 9

Kathy sat in front of the fireplace and watched the small fire slowly burning the newspaper, hoping that the smaller kindling would take so she could start adding larger pieces of wood.

Behind her, Samantha was in the kitchenette at the propane skillet preparing their dinner. The sun had set and it was later than either of them wanted to eat, but they were both starving after a long day of hiking and Samantha didn't want to bring back any of the food they had brought with them.

"Success!" Kathy cheered as she added a smaller log on top of the fire. "Now hopefully that takes."

"Yeah, and then we can get some heat in here." Samantha pulled the sleeves of her sweatshirt down over her hands. The burgers on the skillet began to sizzle.

Kathy sat on the couch in front of the fireplace and draped her arm over the back so she could face her sister. “I’m just glad we got almost everything packed up. Tomorrow, we’ll just need to get dressed and go. I don’t even want to take the time to shower or make breakfast.”

“Great, what a pleasant drive home we’ll have. Smelly and hungry.” Samantha smiled as she flipped the burgers.

“It’s not like you smell like a bed of roses, either. Besides, I’m going to take a shower before I go to bed tonight, so problem solved.”

“I want to leave before daybreak, if possible.”

“Set an alarm,” Kathy said. “Five o’clock. No dawdling in the morning. We get up and go.”

Samantha pulled the burgers off the skillet and set them on a paper plate. “Don’t you think you’re overreacting just a bit? I mean, I got the same creepy vibes from that family, but I think if we leave before they even wake up we’ll be fine.”

“I get the sense that those people are early risers. They’ll notice us leaving.”

“Whatever you say.” Samantha pulled out the pack of hamburger buns, and got the condiments from the fridge. “This is ready.”

Kathy went to the fridge and pulled out the bag of salad they had brought. Other than a few main meals and snacks, they didn’t bring too much food because they didn’t want to worry about bringing the excess back. Seeing as they were eating the last of their food, Kathy deemed their plan a success.

The sisters sat at the small table and ate quietly. The fire in the fireplace had taken off, casting warmth and light into the cabin. Even though they were both desperate to go home, it was a nice, cozy night.

"You know, I had a good day today," Kathy said. "Despite our detour to the crazy house."

Samantha smiled. "Me too. You were right, we needed this weekend for just the two of us as sisters. And it was nice to get away. Even if you had to drag me out of my shell."

Kathy put a hand to her chest and feigned surprised. "What was that? You said I was *right*?"

"Yeah, yeah." Samantha rolled her eyes with another smirk. "But I'm ready to go home. I miss Josh like crazy. And Steven."

Kathy laughed. "Oh yeah. Your *husband*."

"More so Josh, though," Samantha said with a chuckle. "I'm just really ready to be home."

"I know what you mean. I like getting away, but I'm definitely looking forward to going home, taking a hot shower, and getting cozy in my bed."

Samantha began picking up their empty plates. "Well, before we do that, we have to survive another night here. Do you think you can handle one more night?"

Now Kathy rolled her eyes. "Yes, I think we can manage. I'll be unconscious for most of it."

The sisters both cleaned up from dinner. Kathy picked up all the trash and put it in a black garbage bag, which she tied up and put by the door. Samantha cleaned the skillet and made sure the kitchenette looked just as good as it did when they had first arrived.

By the time they finished, the fire in the fireplace was still roaring with life. Kathy plopped on the couch as Samantha took a seat on the other end.

"We're going to need to stop at the dumpster on the way out tomorrow," Kathy said. "Passing by the house is as close to the Fishers as I want to get."

Again, Samantha rolled her eyes. "Well, hopefully they'll still be asleep when we leave in the morning."

Kathy brought her knees up to her chest and hugged them. Her eyes were trained on the burning embers in the fire. "I'm not quite ready for bed yet. And I don't feel like taking a shower just yet."

"The fire feels nice," Samantha said.

They were both quiet as they watched the flames.

"What are you thinking about?" Samantha asked.

Kathy chuckled. "Josh. Apparently he's on both of our minds."

"What about him?"

"He's grown so much. I can see more and more of you in him every day."

Samantha smirked. "Yeah. It's kind of amazing. And kind of

scary. All at the same time. It's like I need to be on my best behavior all the time because he's noticing so much."

"Are you and Steven going to have any more kids?"

"I don't know," Samantha said with a shrug. "We're not *not* trying. If it happens, it happens. If not, that's okay too."

"Now that you have one, the pressure's off to have more?"

"Yeah, I guess. It's like, I wouldn't *mind* more, but I also feel very content with the size of our family, you know?"

Kathy smiled. She hoped that could have her own family someday. But spending most days with Josh now that she'd moved back in was fulfilling her in a way she never had imagined before.

She stretched, raising her hands high above her as she yawned. "Well, I should get in the shower if we're going to leave first thing in the morning."

Samantha's attention turned outside. She shushed her sister as she peered out the window from her perch on the couch.

"What is it?" Kathy asked.

"Don't you hear that?"

"Hear what?" Just as soon as the words left her lips, she heard it.

Barking dogs and men's voices.

CHAPTER 10

"What is that?" Kathy asked as she turned her attention to the window too.

"I don't know." Samantha rose and stepped slowly to the window. "Turn out the light in the kitchen."

Kathy got up and did as she was told, even though she had no idea what was going on. When they killed the lights, the only illumination was from the fireplace, most of which was blocked by the couch.

After a second thought, Kathy rushed to the door and locked it. Shortly after she heard nails scratching on the other side.

She dropped down to the floor, as Samantha did the same under the window. Kathy scooted over until she was sitting side-by-side with her sister.

Outside, they heard a man shout, "Dale, boy, get off the damn door! We don't need no scratches scaring off the next group."

Kathy looked to her sister. She whispered, "What the hell is going on?"

Samantha, meanwhile, sat back against the wall with her eyes closed. She looked perfectly calm, and Kathy could tell that she was fully focused on her mind specialty. Suddenly, her eyes flickered open and worry became evident on her face. "It's the Fishers! They're trying to clear us out of here!"

"Ugh, if they could just wait until morning, we'd do it ourselves."

"I don't think they want us to leave. I think they just want us out of the cabin." Samantha chanced a look behind her and out the window.

Outside, another man's voice called, "Go on and scare them out of there!"

Kathy turned to her sister with panic. "What are we going to do? There's only one exit!"

"All right. Take a deep breath. We're witches."

"They have guns!"

"But we're *witches*," Samantha insisted. "We can outsmart them. We just need to think."

"Let's just cast a spell and go home."

"No. We need to figure out what's going on. Besides, didn't

you hear them? They were talking about the *next* group, meaning they're hoping there will be more. It means that we're not the first. Think about that wallet we found today. Maybe something happened to him. Maybe he was the one who stayed in this cabin before us."

"Well, he's gone, and the crazies are now knocking on *our* door," Kathy said. "Let's just go home, clear our heads, and then come back and—"

"Kathy, it's our jobs as witches to protect people, and that's what I intend to do."

The doorjamb crumbled as the door was kicked in. Kathy shrieked and turned toward the man who appeared in the doorway. Instinct kicked in and soon he was frozen with her magic.

"Nice work. Let's go." Samantha grabbed Kathy's hand and slipped out past the magically-frozen man. Upon closer inspection, she saw it was one of the boys from the pictures in the Fisher house.

Outside, Kathy snatched up the boots she had put by the door as Samantha raced to the car. Both of them made it inside, but when Samantha jammed the keys into the ignition and tried to start it, the car only clicked.

"It's not working!" Samantha cried out.

"Pete? Kurt? What the hell happened to you?" a young man's voice called from the shadows.

"The damn bitches made it to the car!" another voice

sounded. This one was familiar. Jim Fisher.

"What are we going to do?" Kathy asked. "I can't keep freezing them, and if the car's broken then there's no way out of here."

"Run." Samantha's eyes were on the cabin. "We have to run."

"Where?" Kathy looked out the windshield herself. Jim, from his perch on the front porch, was locked into a staring contest with Samantha.

"It doesn't matter. The woods. We just need to get out. One." Samantha pulled the key out of the ignition and slid it into the pocket of her sweatshirt. "Two." She set her hand on the door handle. "Three." She wrenched open the door, just as Jim darted down the stairs.

Coming around the car, Samantha reached for Kathy's hand and sprinted toward the edge of the woods in the opposite direction of the cabin.

The Fishers fired their guns in their direction from behind them, but by then they had made it into the thick of the trees. They heard bullets smacking against tree trunks, and the sisters raced into the darkness, deeper into the woods.

Dogs barked and snarled behind them as well, until Jim Fisher's voice called them back. The sisters weren't naïve enough to think that this was the end.

They were being hunted.

CHAPTER 11

Samantha and Kathy ran for what felt like miles. They weren't following any trails, so everything started to look the same in the woods. It was easy for them to get turned around, but they were simply trying to get *away*.

As they ran, the sound of dogs barking seemed to get further and further away. That was a god sign.

Finally, Samantha stopped and leaned against a tree as she bent over, gasping for breath. She thought she might vomit, right there in the woods. That would surely leave a sign of where they had been and she wondered if the Fishers could somehow use it to track them down.

"You okay?" Kathy rubbed her sister's back in reassurance.

Samantha nodded, but continued to cough. After forcing

herself to take deep, steady breaths, Samantha began to get control of herself again. "Haven't ever run like that." She covered her mouth with her elbow and coughed again.

"Me neither," Kathy said. "I even have a cramp." She turned back and looked in the direction they had come from. No sign of anyone following them, but then, if they were truly being hunted, then there wouldn't be. It didn't mean they weren't being watched. Or tracked. "We can't keep going on like this. We're tired from hiking all day. We need to find somewhere to hide so the dogs can't catch us."

Samantha shook her head and forced another deep breath. "I'm still trying to figure out why the Fishers want us dead in the first place."

"Do you think they figured out that we were witches?"

"How? We haven't used our magic all weekend."

"Yeah, but we've talked about it a few times. Privately."

"I don't think they have hidden cameras or anything like that," Samantha said. "If anything, them knowing we are witches would make them *scared* of us, wouldn't it? I almost wonder if it's because we're women."

"Really?"

"Sure. Think about it. Big macho men. Big guns—and lots of them, I'm sure. Probably had to hold back from calling us *little ladies*." Samantha rolled her eyes. "They probably think we're easy targets, like they can spook us easily."

"Sam, we *are* spooked."

"And we can't let them see that."

"But if they're coming after us because we're women, then how does that explain that guy whose wallet we found? Larry."

Samantha shrugged. "I don't know. That's what I'm trying to sort out. Nothing about these psychos makes any sense to me."

"That's probably a good thing."

The older sister raised her eyebrows. "Yeah. Either way, we need a plan."

Kathy cast a nervous glance backwards. She swore she heard the sound of dogs barking getting louder. "I'm still in favor of casting a spell to get home. Then we can call the police and have them come out and investigate."

"With what proof? And how would we explain that we got all the way back to Erie without a car?" Samantha shook her head. "No. We need to stay here."

"Are you crazy?" Kathy waved her hand back to the sound of dogs—which she *knew* she heard now. "Sam, they're going to *kill* us!"

"I'm thinking about Larry. He has to be the Fishers' previous victim—or target. Maybe he's still alive in the woods somewhere."

"That's a slim chance."

"Then we need to make sure we find his body and give him a proper burial. He deserves that."

Kathy put her hands on her hips. "So you're going to risk your life for someone you don't even know?"

"We're witches. That's what we do."

The younger sister didn't agree the risk was worth the reward. If they *knew* Larry was still alive and needed help, that would be a different story. But risking their lives to save someone who *might* be alive seemed too risky. Especially with Josh back at home, expecting his mom and aunt to return to him safely.

The sound of dogs barking was unmistakable now. Soon the Fishers would be on them with guns waving in their faces. They needed to move.

"We need a plan," Kathy said. "As long as the dogs are chasing us, they'll have our scent. There's nowhere for us to hide *without* using magic."

Samantha pointed down the ravine to the creek. "Water. The dogs will lose our scent if we cross water."

"Sam, that's so dangerous! Not only is it going to be a bitch getting down there, but we'd be sitting ducks if they came to the top of the ravine and shot at us."

"It's the only way out." Samantha turned and started picking a path down the steep slope. "It's either that or die."

Kathy hesitated, but one look back in the direction they had come from made up her mind. The Fishers were gaining on them. They needed to move.

CHAPTER 12

The girls picked their way down the ravine as quickly as they could. The slope was steep, and the fallen leaves and loose rocks made the trip treacherous.

Kathy couldn't help but feel like they had made a bad decision by going down to the creek. Not only was their pace slowed, but if they hurt themselves, they wouldn't ever be able to make up that distance that the Fishers were gaining on them.

The sound of the dogs behind them was like an ominous prelude to the end of their luck so far. It wouldn't take the dogs nearly as long to make it down the ravine. And once the Fishers lined up a good shot, they wouldn't even have to leave their perch at the top of the ravine to stop the girls in their tracks.

Samantha was the first to reach the edge of the creek. Kathy was right behind her. Both of them stood side-by-side and eyed up the distance across. It wasn't very wide, but it was wide enough that they would have to step in the water.

And that was the point, wasn't it? So the dogs would lose their scent and get turned around.

The rustle of leaves above them forced Kathy to step into the water first. Her breath caught when the water filled the old boot. It was ice cold.

"What's the matter?" Samantha asked quietly behind her.

"Cold." But they didn't have time to complain about it, so Kathy pressed on. The small current flowed quietly, but it was powerful enough to cause Kathy to momentarily lose her balance. She put her arms out wide to steady herself as her body bent at the waist to regain her balance.

She found her footing again and crossed to the other side, grateful to get out of the water. Worries about hypothermia were pushed aside as she turned back across the creek and ushered her sister forward.

In the distance, they could hear the dogs barking, getting closer. They needed to move quickly. Especially if they were going to get back up the other side of the ravine and lose themselves in the woods again.

Samantha glanced back up to the top of the ravine, then looked across to her sister. She carefully stepped into the water, gasping at the cold just as Kathy had, and quickly crossing the gently-moving water.

Halfway across, her foot slipped and she let out a yelp of pain.

Kathy stared, wide-eyed. She looked up to the top, then back to Samantha. "Come on!"

"I twisted my ankle," Samantha said. "And my foot is stuck!"

Sucking in a deep breath, Kathy stepped back into the water and winced at the frigid temperature. She stepped carefully on the slippery rocks beneath until she reached her sister. Grabbing ahold of her arm to steady them both, she held Samantha pulled her foot out of the space between the boulder and the muck where it had been lodged.

Samantha let out another cry of pain.

"Shh!" Kathy insisted.

"I can't help it." Now with her foot free, the sisters tried to cross the back to the other side, but as soon as Samantha put weight on her foot, her leg crumpled with pain and she clung to Kathy to keep her from crashing into the water. "Ow! Ow! Ow!"

"You can't walk on it?"

Through gritted teeth, Samantha replied, "*OW!*"

"They're down by the creek!" the Fishers called from above.

"Okay, okay! Lean on me." Kathy pulled her sister's arm around her shoulder and helped her cross back to the shore. "You okay?" Kathy saw the Fishers standing at the top of the ravine. One of the dogs already started making its way down toward the creek. "Never mind! Let's go!"

Samantha again clung to her sister as she hopped on her one

good foot. Meanwhile, Donovan Fisher pointed his rifle at them from above and fired. The bullet struck the spot where the girls had been moments before.

"Sam, we have to *move*!" Kathy groaned as she tried to drag her sister along.

"I'm *trying*!"

The gunshots continued to fire as the sisters made their way alongside the creek bed. They didn't have the time or the ability to make their way back up the other side, not with Samantha's injury and not without completely exposing themselves to the Fishers. Kathy considered freezing them again, but she would need to turn and concentrate on them, and she doubted she'd even be in range to get them all. And revealing her powers was not something she wanted to do just yet. Not until they were closer to actually getting home. For now, they just needed to survive.

Which meant that running was their only option.

Except, with Samantha limping and hopping along, their pursuit was anything but a "run."

"Come on, Sam! Let's go!" Kathy bit back more words that sprung to her mind from a place of fear. Even with all of the magical things they had faced in their lives, this was by far the most intense.

There was a fallen tree blocking their way. It crossed over the middle of the creek, but the root ball was still intact. The tree came up to their bellies. Too high to climb over with Samantha's foot, but too low to climb under.

"I'm going to lift you over," Kathy said.

"And how am I going to catch myself?"

Wood chips flew into their faces as a bullet was lodged deep into the fallen tree. The girls let out a cry and covered their faces.

When Kathy turned back to get over the log, she saw a man standing there, extending his hand.

"Here!" he said. "I'll help you over!"

Samantha hesitated, but Kathy felt more wood chips pelting her face and she hoisted her sister up. The man took Samantha on the other side and pulled her over. Kathy hopped over on her own and the three of them ducked behind the log for cover.

"Who the hell are you?" Kathy asked the man. This was the first opportunity she had to really get a good look at him. His hair was greasy and matted. He had dirt all over his face and ends. And he smelled of sweat. His camouflage clothing seemed stiff and in need of a good wash. To sum it all up, Kathy thought that he looked like hell. In a cute sort of way.

"And how do we know we can trust you?" Samantha added.

"I think the words you're looking for are, 'thank you.'" The man gave a cheshire grin, then winced as another bullet hit the log. "They're going to keep shooting until they can chew up this tree enough and hit one of us. Either that, or they're going to have two guys shoot while another two come down further along the ravine and shoot us from this side."

"So what do you suggest we do?" Kathy asked. "My sister's hurt."

"I see that. But we're still going to have to run. We're just going to have to wait for the perfect moment to make our escape."

Kathy turned and looked back over the log. She put up her hands and froze them—three men, from what she could see.

The bullets stopped.

"How did you...?" the man asked.

"No time to talk," Kathy said. "You told us we have to run. Help me with Samantha?"

"I can get it myself," Samantha said.

"But it'd be faster if I helped." The man scooped her up in both of his arms and started walking along the creek bed.

"Where are we going?" Kathy asked as she followed behind.

"Out of the ravine. Trust me, I've been on the run from these psychos for a week now. If they know they have you scared, they're going to keep coming at you until they kill you."

"But what do they want from us?" Samantha asked.

"They want to hunt us. And if we don't get out of this ravine, it'll be like shooting fish in a barrel for them."

CHAPTER 13

- 1985 -

"Donovan! Get your ass outta bed, boy!" Rodney's voice hollered into Donovan's bedroom, waking him instantly. "Help me get this damn refrigerator out into the yard. Your Uncle Jim is on his way over with another one for us."

Donovan groaned at the abrupt end to his slumber. He lay in bed and yawned, stretching his arms and legs out away from the core of his body. He hadn't gotten much sleep. He and his cousins were out late on a hunting trip. This time it was a fox they were after. Uncle Jim had nicked it with his pistol after it tried to get the drying deer meat hanging in the barn.

Apparently, the bullet wound to the back hadn't done much because the fox, while it moved relatively slowly, had managed to travel pretty far. And while the cousins thought that it'd get stuck in one of the traps they had set closer to the house, the creature had managed to travel to the back of the property before getting caught in one of the traps.

It took the boys hours to find the animal. At that point, they were all so exhausted—and annoyed—from searching into the middle of the night that they took their frustrations out on it. And when it tried to fight back? That's what really did the animal in.

The bedroom door swung open again, bringing with it the blinding light of the morning. The smell of cigarette smoke told Donovan it was his father who entered.

"I *told* you, boy!" Rodney's fingers gripped Donovan's hair and jerked him up, pulling him out of bed. "Get up and help me, you worthless piece of shit! Goddammit, you're so *lazy*!"

Donovan pushed his father away, but the grip on his hair was strong.

The effort didn't go unnoticed.

"You trying to fight like a man, huh? You don't have what it takes." Rodney leaned in close to his son's face. "You need to treat your father with some respect, *boy*."

Donovan pushed his father again. He was successful this time. He fell to the floor, cigarette still propped in the corner of his mouth between his lips.

He wasn't down for long before Donovan pounced on him and wrapped his hands around Rodney's throat. His grip was strong, fueled by anger—and embarrassment. The cigarette fell from Rodney's lips as they struggled. He brought his hands up to try to pry off Donovan's, but the more he flailed, the faster his face turned blue.

"Hey!" Gretchen came into the room. "Get your hands off your father!" She kicked Donovan in the side. Her foot made contact with his kidney, sending immediate pain up his spine.

Donovan rolled off and onto the floor. Now he was struggling to catch his breath.

"You okay, honey?" Gretchen helped her husband off the floor. He was barely to his feet before she turned back on Donovan. "And you! What the hell do you think you're doing, putting your hands on the man who helps feed you? You have no right! Such a selfish little prick, you are. You think you can push around your old man and then what? You're going to be a tough guy? You're not. You're pathetic. You're twenty years old and still living in the same bedroom where you used to piss the bed in. I thought we'd be rid of you by now."

By now, Donovan had managed to get a few deep breaths back into his lungs and he could feel his strength returning. Using the wall for support, he got to his feet, but another blow from his mother sent him right back down to the floor.

The kicks came in such quick succession that Donovan knew that both of his parents had turned on him. All he could do was cower and use his arm to protect his head.

But the kicks still made contact with his skull. More than

once he felt their feet collide with his head. One blow in particular filled his mouth with blood. The next moment, he felt one of his teeth fall out and he spit it out on the carpet.

And then the kicking stopped. Donovan chanced a glance up and saw Uncle Jim pulling both Rodney and Gretchen back by their shirt collars. One-by-one, he tossed them out of the trailer.

Scrambling to his feet, Donovan raced to the doorway, but then had to lean on it for support as his head spun.

"You two can get the hell out of here," Jim told them calmly.

"You can't throw me out," Rodney countered. "You may own the land, but I own the trailer. That's private property you're standing in. You're trespassing!"

"Get out of here, or I'll kill you." Jim was still calm. As if they were talking about the weather and not their mortality.

Despite the peaceful tone, Donovan still saw the fear cross the faces of both of his parents.

"Come on. You wouldn't kill your own brother," Rodney pleaded.

Jim pulled the pistol from his hip and pointed it at them. "I'll shoot you both right here if you don't believe me."

Rodney was the first to run, leaving his wife behind. When she saw he was gone, she turned and took off after him. Both of them disappearing into the woods.

Jim watched them go, then turned to his nephew. "You okay, son?"

Donovan nodded slightly. His head was pounding too much for a proper nod, but he didn't want to appear weak in front of his uncle. "I will be."

"We'll get you back to the house and Aunt Sue will get you cleaned up good as new. But first, I need you to get dressed while I call your cousins. We're going hunting."

CHAPTER 14

Kathy helped Samantha limp along as they followed behind the man. They had made it out of the ravine and were walking deeper in the woods on the other side. The uneven terrain wasn't helping Samantha's ankle, but she was able to put some weight on it now, which made their progress slow, but still faster than it had been.

Their rescuer walked several feet ahead of them. He had told them it was probably a good idea for them to linger behind so that he could scope out their path, but Kathy wondered if the real reason was that he didn't want questions. Or he wanted to keep them at a distance so he could kill them. The jury was still out on his real motive.

Kathy?

Samantha's voice pinged in her head and Kathy jerked upright and looked over at her sister, who frowned and shook her head vigorously.

"Is there a problem?" The man stopped and looked back at them.

"No problem," Kathy blurted, perhaps too loudly. "Just lost my footing for a second."

The man put a finger to his lips. "Shh. Best to move quietly. Watch your step from now on."

Kathy nodded and waited for him to turn back around before they all kept moving again.

It's me, Samantha.

The voice pinged in Kathy's head again. She hated it when her sister used her telepathic abilities with her. It was such an invasion of privacy. But in this circumstance, she was grateful to have a private way to communicate.

Yeah, I got that, Kathy thought, knowing that her sister would read it.

What's your take on this guy?

Kathy looked ahead and watched as he moved through the woods quickly but carefully. *Not sure yet. You have any inklings about him?*

It's hard to get a read, Samantha thought back. *He doesn't seem like a threat.*

Have you considered that he's one of the Fishers? Kathy thought. *Maybe he's a decoy, used to let our guard down and lead us right into a trap.*

Samantha shook her head. *No, but I also haven't gotten any bad vibes from him. Not like I did when we met Jim and the other Fishers. But this guy does look familiar.*

Do you know him?

I don't think so. I can't quite place why he looks so familiar, but he does.

Kathy helped Samantha step over another fallen log—smaller this time, half rotten and much more manageable to navigate. But it still took Samantha a while as she shifted her body weight from one foot to another, forcing her to put more pressure on her injured ankle than she wanted to.

Once they crossed it, Kathy thought back, *Well, whether or not he looks familiar, I think it's stupid to blindly trust him.*

I agree, Samantha thought. *But he did help us out of the ravine and away from the Fishers. For the moment, he's our best shot at surviving this nightmare. At least until I can give me ankle a rest.*

We could always cast a spell, Kathy said.

And leave him high and dry? He saved us, Kathy.

Kathy glanced over at her sister. *Yeah, only because you refused to cast a spell when the Fishers first chased us out of our cabin. We could've been sitting at home right now.*

And would you have slept well knowing that Larry and this guy were out here being hunted by a family of murderers?

We don't know for sure that they're murderers.

But the clues all point to that, Samantha pointed out. *We need to stay. It's our duty as witches.*

Kathy held back from letting her mind wander to Steven and Josh, whom Samantha also had an obligation to.

The sad look Samantha gave her told Kathy that she wasn't as good at hiding her thoughts as she thought.

The man ahead stopped suddenly and looked back at the girls, waiting for them to catch up.

"Did you see something?" Samantha asked him.

"No," he said. "It's been quiet for a while now and we're pretty far out from the main house on the Fisher property. I think they've given up on us for the night."

"How can you be sure?" Kathy asked.

"They don't usually like to hunt at night," he explained. "Not unless they're starting a hunt. They like to scare out their victims on the last night of their stay, after they're tired and ready to say goodbye to the outdoors. It puts the Fishers at an advantage that they use to chase them down and—"

Samantha raised her hand to stop him. "Okay, I think we can connect the dots. That sounds exactly like what the Fishers did with us when they pushed us out of our cabin."

The man nodded. "Yup. You certainly aren't the first ones to fall into their trap."

"How do you know?" Kathy asked.

"You're another one of their victims," Samantha said before he could answer. Then, as realization kicked in, she added, "I saw you on a missing persons flyer back at the gas station in town!"

The man's face turned down. "Yeah. I'm Rick. I was on a hunting trip with my friend Clay last week."

"You can hunt out here with the trails?" Kathy asked. "And so close to the National Forest?"

Rick shrugged. "That's what the Fishers told us. Funny how their stories change to fit whatever narrative suits them best, isn't it? They never showed us the hiking trails. In fact, they directed us away from them and said that they hunt on the property all the time and as long as we stayed five hundred feet from any cabin or other structure that we'd be fine to hunt."

"So you were chased out like us?" Samantha asked.

"It was our last night." Rick turned his head down and pushed away the leaves at his feet that were concealing a small rock. "We were going to leave in the morning. Didn't get anything, but we'd had a good time. The Fishers sent their dogs in after us, chased us out. They started firing, but I don't think they were really trying to hit us. Just trying to scare us. We ran into the woods." He took in a deep breath and looked the girls in the eyes. "The Fishers stole all of our weapons. Completely wiped out everything we had brought, as if we were never there."

"How do you know?" Samantha asked.

"I chanced a trip back a few days later," he explained. "We were staying in the last cabin, down by the creek. It was the furthest from their house, so I thought it was safe."

Kathy looked over at her sister. They had thought the same thing when they had first arrived. "That was our cabin too." She pointed down to her sodden boots. "I found these on the front porch. Are these yours? The Fishers must've forgotten them when they cleared out your things."

Rick cleared his throat and looked down again. "Uh…they were Clay's."

The three of them were silent as the weight of the past tense sunk in.

"He didn't make it, did he?" Samantha asked quietly.

Rick shook his head. "No, he didn't." Again, he cleared his throat, then pointed a few feet behind them. "I, uh—I found a hiding place that I've been using to sleep in each night. It's protected from the weather. Not very warm, depending on the night, but it has protected me for the last week. It'll be tight with the three of us, but we'll have to manage. We'll do better with sleep than without."

Do we trust this stranger to sleep with him for one night? Kathy thought. She tried to project it loudly enough for her sister to telepathically "hear" it.

We're going to have to, Samantha pinged back.

Rick pointed to their legs. "You'll need to get out of those wet clothes. Otherwise, you'll catch hypothermia overnight."

Samantha offered a disgusted look. "Absolutely not! I'm not going to take my clothes off and sleep naked with you!"

"You will if you want to save your extremities," he said. "We're in survival mode. All humility needs to be tossed out the window. Besides, I'm not asking you to sleep naked. I have some dry clothes at the shelter that I've collected from other visitors in the last week. You can wear those until yours dry out."

"You mean clothes you've *stolen*?" Kathy clarified.

He stared at her intensely, which she held without backing down. "And if I hadn't, you'd have to sleep naked, just like your sister here was afraid of. Like I said, all humility needs to be thrown away if you want to get out of here alive."

The two studied each other for a moment before Rick turned and started off toward the shelter. "Come on. It's late enough as it is and we'll need to get an early start if we want to find a way out of here."

CHAPTER 15

Kathy crawled out of the covered hole that Rick had allowed them to sleep in overnight. The muscles in her back felt knotted, her hair was a tangled mess, and her skin felt sticky from the dried sweat after their midnight sprint through the woods.

She was miserable.

She only wished she had taken a shower the night before like she had wanted to. Before the Fishers scared them out. Maybe then she wouldn't feel so sticky with sweat. Then again, there was a chance that she'd be chased into the woods completely naked if the Fishers came while she was in the shower.

Raising her hands above her head, she reached up, then

down to touch her toes, trying to stretch out her muscles. She held each pose for several seconds before moving on to the next.

"Rough night?" Samantha asked behind her.

"Ugh, I need a massage," Kathy complained. "And a nice hot shower. Oh, and I'm hungry."

"Well, we'll be lucky if even see home again." Samantha propped herself against a pine tree to stretch out her ankle.

"Don't talk like that. How's your leg?"

"Still tender, but I should be able to walk on it today." Samantha put some extra weight on it and cringed at the dull ache. "What I really need is to ice it and elevate it."

"Well, I can't help with the ice, but I can feed you." The rustling of leaves and the sound of Rick's voice scared both witches. He carried several fish on a string. "Went down to the creek this morning to check for any signs of the Fishers. Doesn't look like they made their way down the ravine, like I suspected. While I was down there I figured I might as well get us something to eat." He raised his morning catch. "All I need to do is fry them up!"

Kathy made a face. She wasn't a huge fan of fish, but her grumbling stomach told her not to be picky. Not in their circumstances.

He pointed in the opposite direction. "I'm going to go about a half-mile, mile away to start the fire so we can keep this place a secret. I suggest you girls clear out of here sooner than later. Oh, and you can probably put your own clothes back on now that they're dry."

The girls both looked down at themselves. Kathy wore a baggy pair of sweatpants that Rick had nabbed from another victim in Cabin 8—she wondered if they were Larry's—and Samantha wore a pair of men's jeans that were quite baggy on her. Both of them had on oversized flannels that helped keep them warm over the chilly October night.

"The shoes might take longer to dry," Rick added. "But I think for today you'll be okay. Looks like it'll be decent weather. Anyway, I'll see you once you're changed and have a chance to catch up."

The sisters watched him walk away, making sure he was fully out of sight without the possibility of sneaking up on them again. When Kathy was sure he was gone, she turned back to the shelter and pulled out her own pair of jeans.

"I'm still not sure if we should trust him." Kathy slipped out of the sweatpants and felt the chill hit her bare legs.

"I think we can." Samantha did the same, although the jeans she'd been wearing didn't take much encouragement to drop to her knees.

"You weren't so sure last night," Kathy said. "What changed your mind?"

"The fact that I still haven't gotten any bad vibes from him. He seems genuine in his efforts to help us." Samantha pulled her own jeans on and zipped them up, then sat on the leafy ground to pull her boots back on.

“You think he’s telling us the whole truth?”

“Well, no. I think he’s hiding something about the disappearance of his friend, but, in general, I think we can trust him. At least, under the circumstances.”

Kathy pulled her pant legs over the top of the borrowed boots that she had just finished lacing up. “Either way, we need to start getting answers from *somebody* if we’re going to get back home in one piece.”

“Agreed.”

Now dressed, the sisters started off in the direction that Rick had gone off in. It took them about thirty minutes to find him. They were slowed down by Samantha’s ankle, although she moved much faster than she had the night before, and then they needed to follow the direction of the smoke back to its source to locate the fire.

“You know, that smoke smell carries quite a distance,” Samantha offered when they walked up to Rick cooking up their fish.

“Nothing we can do about that. It is what it is.” Rick kept his eyes on their meal, occasionally looking up and scoping out the wilderness.

“You’re not worried they’ll spot us?” Kathy didn’t have to define who “they” were.

This time, he turned to look at her. “We’re miles away from the Fisher’s main house. Even if they ventured out this far, we’d be long gone by the time they got here. I think we're safe."

"Famous last words," Samantha mumbled.

"Possibly," he said, "but sometimes we have to take risks."

The sisters remained quiet at that. They were taking a risk at the moment by following Rick's lead.

"These should be done in a few minutes," he said. "It took me longer than I anticipated to start the fire this morning."

"You're not a pro yet?" Samantha took a seat on a log adjacent to him.

"Hardly." Rick used a stick to turn the fish. They were skewered on another stick and propped up over the fire. "That was always Clay's expertise whenever we went camping."

Kathy took a seat beside her sister. "Are you ever going to tell us what really happened to him?"

Rick smirked, but studied the fire. "I suppose I will once you explain how you were able to stop the Fishers—and their bullets—all with the flick of your hand." He turned toward them. "It was as if time had stopped for them and them alone."

Kathy's heart beat a little faster. She looked to Samantha for help.

"You saw that, even in the dark, huh?" Samantha asked him.

He nodded. "I did. And let me point out that now we both know we're keeping secrets from each other. And yet, if we're going to make it home from this camping trip from hell, then we're going to need to trust each other. Even with these secrets we're keeping."

"I'm sor—" Kathy started but Rick put up his hand as his eyes darted out into the thick of the woods.

"We're being watched," he said in a low, quiet voice.

Kathy tried to listen to what he had heard—was it the dogs returning? Footsteps in the leaves? A snap of a branch? She heard nothing.

Slowly, Rick got up and moved carefully but quickly in a crouched position. "Guard the food."

The sisters watched him disappear into the trees, then Kathy shot to her feet and mimicked Rick's movement.

"Where are you going?" Samantha whisper-shouted to her sister.

"Just stay there!" Kathy caught up to Rick, who shot her a dirty look for not listening to his direction. Well, if he thought they were just going to blindly follow his lead, then he was sadly mistaken.

Rick put a finger to his lips, then motioned that they were going to travel a long way around from where he heard the intruder into their makeshift camp.

He directed Kathy to make a wide loop around in the opposite direction of him. They'd meet up behind the intruder and sneak up on them.

This time, Kathy did what he asked, only because she wanted to get a good vantage point herself. As she came around at the wide angle, she saw Rick twenty feet away from her hiding behind another tree.

When he motioned for them to move forward, she still wasn't sure what they were about to come up on. She presumed an animal, but what animal would be that small that she couldn't see it on the other side of an overgrown bush? A fox? A coyote? A raccoon?

But when Rick finally sprung on their uninvited visitor, Kathy saw for herself why she hadn't been able to see what was on the other side.

It was a little girl, no more than eight. And she looked terrified.

CHAPTER 16

The girl jumped when she saw Kathy and Rick. After only a fraction of a second's hesitation, she darted from her hiding place and took off deeper into the woods.

"Hey!" Kathy called after her. "Are you hungry?"

Just as she suspected, that got the girl's attention. She stopped and peered back carefully at Kathy.

"We can share some of our food with you."

Behind Kathy, Rick grumbled. "Barely caught enough for the three of us, but sure."

Kathy looked back at him. "She's a little girl. What are we supposed to do? Let her starve?" Turning back to the girl, she raised her voice and asked, "What's your name?"

The girl took a few careful steps back toward them. "Crystal."

"That's a pretty name. I'm Kathy, and this is Rick. How old are you, Crystal?"

"I'm eight. I'm really hungry." She started to whimper. "I don't even like fish, but I'm *so hungry*."

Kathy closed the distance between them and knelt down in front of the girl. "I don't really like fish that much, either. But we have to keep our bodies strong if we're going to make it home safely."

Crystal began to cry completely now and she leaned into Kathy's embrace.

"What's wrong?" Kathy's tone was sympathetic.

The words tumbled out of the girl in a breathless recount of her tragedies. "I don't know where my mom and dad are. After the bad men chased us out of our cabin, my mom and me went one way and my dad went another way and then my mom told me to stay hidden while she went and looked for my dad, but she hasn't been back yet." Her lower lip jutted out and she looked down at the ground as her shoulders shook with sobs.

Kathy pulled the girl in for another hug. It suddenly hit her that she'd seen Crystal before. Or rather, a picture of her. The one of the family from Larry's wallet.

"Come on," Kathy encouraged. "Let's go back to the fire. My sister, Samantha, is probably done cooking the fish. We'll feel better after we eat. Don't worry, we'll protect you."

As she led Crystal back to the fire, Kathy glanced at Rick and saw him brooding as he followed.

"Who's this?" Samantha asked when Kathy ushered Crystal to sit on a log.

"This is Crystal," Kathy spoke for the girl. "She's looking for her parents. They were also chased out of the cabin, like us. I told her she could share some of our food."

Samantha smiled at Crystal. "Hello! I'm Samantha. I just pulled the fish off the fire a few minutes ago, so it should be cool enough to eat now."

Their meal was sitting on a rock, splayed out with the scales and bones already picked off by Samantha.

"We'll take care of you," Samantha said. "Until we find your parents, that is."

Rick cleared his throat and grumbled, "That might not happen."

Both witches shot daggers at him and he turned away from them to keep an eye on their surroundings.

"Don't listen to him," Samantha told the girl. "Trust me, I'm a mom. There's nothing that will keep a parent from their child. You just have to be strong until we find them. Do you think you can do that?"

Crystal nodded and her eyes traveled to the fish.

As Samantha and Crystal started eating, Kathy turned her back to face Rick.

Lowering her voice, she asked, "So what's the plan?"

"What do you mean?" His eyes scanned the brush around them.

"I realize we don't really know much about each other, but let me tell you this: I hate camping. So the idea of spending yet *another* night in a hole in the ground doesn't really appeal to me." It was impossible to keep the sarcasm out of her voice.

"And you think *I* enjoy it?"

Kathy shrugged. "I'm not really sure. And, truth be told, it doesn't matter. The fact is, we need to find a way out of the woods. More importantly, I'd like to make sure we stop the Fishers from hurting anyone else. With our group alone, there's a track record of them doing this at *least* three times in the last week. How many others have they succeeded with? How many more will there be after us if we don't stop them? Would you be able to sleep comfortably in your warm bed back home knowing that you didn't do something to prevent more pain and suffering like this?"

Rick stood with his arms crossed. His face was stoic, but Kathy could tell that she was appealing to his humanity. "Sounds like you have some ideas. Let's hear them."

"Well, I don't have anything concrete," she admitted, "but I've been thinking the best way to stop them in their tracks is to hit them where they least expect us to show up: back at their house."

CHAPTER 17

"Wow, we're screwed." Kathy crossed her arms as she looked down at the scant few options they had for weapons.

After they had eaten breakfast, Rick had led the group to another spot in the woods several miles away. Under the cover of two fallen trees and cleverly-placed piles of leaves, he had been able to hide his cavalry of fighting gear that he'd collected over the last week.

The sisters were not impressed.

"What do you mean?" Rick asked. "We have enough for the three of us. And even if we had more, I wouldn't want to give her one anyway." He pointed to Crystal, who sat on the fallen tree and watched the adults converse.

"She'll need to be able to protect herself," Samantha pointed out. "No matter her age. It's not like we're in an everyday situation here. The rules can bend a bit."

"And what are you going to do when she hurts herself?" he countered.

"Well, we'd have to guide her with it." Samantha rolled her eyes. "Obviously. She's eight, yes, but she's not dumb." Looking over at Crystal, Samantha asked, "Have you ever pretended to sword-fight with any cousins or anyone else your age, sweetie?"

The little girl nodded and smiled. "Yeah! It's a lot of fun! And I always win."

Samantha held out her hand to the girl but looked up at Rick. "See? She's already got some experience."

"Please, you think that'll be enough to go up against some psychos? They'll kill us all while laughing in our faces!"

"It's the best we can do with this trash." Kathy knelt down next to the poor-man's arsenal. There were several sturdy sticks that had been whittled down to a point. A couple sheets of metal that had been ripped so that there was a sharp edge, the lower half protected by a scrap of flannel that had been tied around the makeshift handle. And then there were the rocks of varying sizes that sat together in a pile.

"Hey! I worked hard to make these!" Rick said.

"I'm sure you did," Samantha said. "And it's better than nothing, but following your own argument you used when we were talking about Crystal, do you honestly think that these can compete with the *guns* the Fishers have? Not to mention their dogs?"

Rick shrugged. "It's all we have to work with. Unless the two of you have some secrets up your sleeves that can help us."

The sisters exchanged looks. They didn't like that Rick knew about their powers. Especially when they weren't fully convinced that they could trust him.

"Would you mind keeping an eye on Crystal?" Kathy asked Rick. "My sister and I need to talk privately."

He put up his hands in surrender and turned to his collected stash.

Samantha and Kathy both walked through the rustling leaves, putting enough distance between them and Rick so that they couldn't be overheard. Samantha leaned on her little sister for support with her weak ankle, which gave them a perfect excuse to have their heads close together and to speak in whispers.

"Did you tell him that we're witches?" Samantha asked.

"No!" Kathy replied. "But he's not dumb. Obviously he knows something. I mean, he already asked us about me freezing the Fishers yesterday."

"Yeah, that was kind of dumb on your part."

"Well, otherwise you'd be dead right now, so I think it was warranted. You *could* say 'thank you.'"

"I'll save that for when we're home safe and sound," Samantha said. "If we ever get there."

"I told you to stop talking like that," Kathy snapped. "Besides, I don't think it's a bad idea."

"To what? Shoot me?"

"No! To use our magic against the Fishers."

Samantha shook her head. "I don't know, Kathy. As far as we know, the Fishers aren't magical."

"So?"

"So we'd be misusing our powers by creating an unfair advantage."

Kathy narrowed her eyes. "Sam, this isn't a friendly game of chess here. This is our lives that they're threatening. And Rick and Crystal's. *And* whoever else the Fishers have scheduled to stay here in the future. Besides, *they* created the unfair advantage when they started *shooting* at us!"

"Okay, yes, they're in the wrong. I get that. But I still don't know if it's the right thing to do."

"Sam, they're hunting us for *sport*. Us. Real life humans here. Not deer so they can have meat for the winter. They're chasing us because it's *fun* for them. They're crazy. This isn't the time to take the moral high road."

Samantha sighed and looked back at Rick and Crystal. "I know. You're right. This isn't a normal situation. But it still doesn't sit well with me."

Kathy tucked her sister's hair back out of her face. "And

that's what makes you a good person. But I'd rather be alive than dead."

"Me too. And I guess it's probably best that we shift to the offensive, if we're ever going to make it home alive."

CHAPTER 18

- 1985 -

Pete and Kurt were coming in from the opposite side of the property. That way, the four of them could trap Rodney and Gretchen in the middle of the woods to make the execution.

Donovan followed Uncle Jim as they ran between the trees, jumping over fallen logs, rocks, and trying to keep steady footing amid the rocky terrain. His heart was racing for reasons other than his pace. He knew what it meant when Uncle Jim said they were on a "hunting" trip. That word had taken on new meaning in the last couple years, mostly because of Donovan's own interest in making dying things suffer.

But could he do that to his own parents? He was about to find out.

Amidst the fallen leaves of the forest floor, Donovan spotted his mother lying on the ground. One quick look in his uncle's direction confirmed that he saw her too. They slowed their pace as they approached.

"The son of a bitch left me!" She reached for her ankle. "Donovan. Help your mother up. I twisted my ankle."

Donovan stood where he was. Despite everything, he was in no mood to *help* his mother. Not when she had just been kicking the crap out of him.

"Don't talk to him," Jim said.

Gretchen looked over at him and cowered away.

Sometimes, Donovan wondered if his uncle could kill from the look on his face alone.

"Jim. We've been family for years! You're like a brother to me. Think of all the holidays we've shared together. The times we've watched each other's kids. Your kids are like brothers to my son. We're family. You can't do this to family."

"When you decided to harm this boy, you made the decision that we're no longer family," Jim said. "Not anymore." He pulled the pistol from its holster on his hip.

Donovan held his breath. His eyes flickered between his uncle and his mother, both of whom were locked in an intense stare.

Then Jim turned to his nephew. "Donovan, would you like to do the honors? It was you who she disrespected. Whose trust she betrayed."

Donovan raised his hand to take the gun, but hesitated before he could actually take it.

"It's okay," Jim encouraged. "You know how to fire one of these. I've shown you."

"Donovan, don't do this! I'm your mother!" Gretchen called from the ground. "My sweet baby boy, please don't do this. I'm sorry! I never should've hurt you like that! You're my angel. I love you."

Did she, though? Is that what it was when she took his father's side in the middle of their fight and not his? Was it love when she started kicking him, knocking out a tooth? Was it love when she ignored him, called him worthless, and wished that she had been "rid" of him?

And did Donovan even love her? Other than allowing him to stay in that crappy trailer—out of obligation, no less—what had she ever done for him to show her love? To prove that he mattered to her? She stopped showing interest in him a long time ago. She never made him dinner, never asked how his day was, and sometimes days would pass where she didn't even talk to him. Uncle Jim, on the other hand, taught him things. How to hunt. How to shoot a gun. How to be a man. How to take care of himself without having to rely on anyone else. Uncle Jim was more of a parent to Donovan than Rodney and Gretchen were.

"You're a hypocrite," Jim said, suddenly angry. "You didn't think he was so perfect when you were kicking the shit out of him. Think of that as you're burning in hell." He raised the gun and fired. Gretchen's body fell to the ground, limp.

Donovan stared wide-eyed, then turned to his uncle and tried to swallow to clear his dry throat.

Jim put the gun back in his side holster. "Don't ever hesitate on a hunting trip. I thought I told you that."

He could do nothing but nod and try to swallow again, but his mouth had gone so dry.

"We need to go find your cousins." Jim walked on past Gretchen's limp body. "We're still hunting."

CHAPTER 19

The four of them walked until the first hints of darkness began to settle in. Rick had led them around the Fisher property, showing them the lay of the land that he had uncovered in the last week. If things went bad for them and they needed to run—or worse, if they were chased—then he wanted all of them to know their way around the woods.

They knew they were getting close when they heard the dogs barking echoing through the trees. Immediately, Kathy had flashbacks to being chased out of the cabin. But, she decided to trust that Rick wasn't just handing them over to the Fishers. She only hoped that her trust wasn't misplaced.

Finally, once they had begun to head toward the Fisher house, Rick rerouted them to the creek. Using the whittled sticks Rick had fashioned himself, they each stood barefoot in the cold water and waited patiently for the fish to come around.

It was Rick's way of showing Crystal how to use a real weapon. Not that she—or the sisters—were successful at catching their dinner.

After they had enough fish for a meal, they dried off their feet, put their shoes and boots back on, and traveled another half mile away from the creek.

"This is a good place to stop," Rick declared once they were far enough away from the water—and the Fisher house. "I'll get started on the fire. You girls want to start skinning the fish?" He pulled a large pocket knife out and offered it to them.

Kathy looked at the fish laid out on the rock and made a face. "Um…I'll pass."

Samantha rolled her eyes, sat down on a nearby rock—with some help now that the swelling in her leg had grown again after being on her feet all day—and got to work.

"I'm tired." Crystal leaned against Kathy as they both sat against a tree.

"I know, sweetie." Kathy ran her fingers through the girl's hair absently. She was impressed with the eight-year-old, who kept up with three adults for the whole day with minimal complaining. And all on an empty stomach. Before they had stopped, Kathy could even feel herself growing agitated from her exhaustion and her hunger.

"You did good today," Samantha said as she filleted the scales off the fish.

"Only a little more walking," Rick added. "I don't like to sleep and eat in the same place."

Kathy looked up into the gray sky beyond the trees. She wasn't sure what kind of shelter they would be able to find at this hour, but she hoped it was something. The air was already turning cold and she didn't want to spend the night out in the open, nor did she think that Crystal's little body could handle it. Not if they expected her to keep up with them another day and, possibly, fight for her life.

"Fire's started," Rick said after another few minutes. "Give it a little bit to heat up and then we can hang the fish over it."

"Do we need to get sticks to prop up the food?" Samantha asked.

"I've already got some." Crystal carried over a handful that she had been absently collecting from around her.

"You want to help me put it all together?" Samantha asked.

"Sure." Crystal extracted herself from her place next to Kathy and sat in front of Samantha while they constructed a system to hold the fish over the fire.

Kathy stood and joined Rick a few feet away from the fire. He was looking out into the woods.

"See anything?" she asked.

"No." His eyes traveled around them in a circle. "And that's a good thing. But I still don't like it that they've been quiet today."

"Didn't you say they'd want us to be scared?" she asked.

"Overnight. They usually come out and hunt them down at the first break of day." His head remained on a swivel. "But we've gone a whole day and still no sign of them. That's not typical."

"How do you know that's usually their plan? And how do we know they haven't been out looking for us and we've just been avoiding them?"

"The sound of gunshots travel far. And those bastards have egos bigger than their guns. They wouldn't let us go so easily. Not to mention the dogs would alert us. And the fact that we haven't seen *any* sign of the Fishers tells me they have something else planned for us."

"Like what?"

"I don't know. But I think we need to stand watch tonight," he suggested. "We'll take shifts so we can all get our rest."

"Not Crystal." Kathy shook her head. "She can sleep through the night."

Rick nodded. "Yeah, that's a good idea."

"What's that noise?" Crystal asked from beside the fire.

The three adults looked at each other, then looked around. They fell silent, the only sound the rustling of the leaves by the wind and the popping of the fire.

Then, Kathy heard it. Footsteps in the leaves.

Crystal let out an ear-piercing scream that was quickly muffled by Samantha's hand.

It wasn't until the coyote was nearly on them that Kathy saw it. The animal rushed to the fish laid out on the rock. Just as it was about to grab it, Rick hurled several rocks at it.

The beast didn't like that and lunged at Rick, pinning him to the ground and going for his neck. Rick managed to push against the creature's chest to keep it from ripping his throat out with its teeth, but he was struggling.

Instinct kicked in and Kathy froze the scene. Bringing her foot up, she delivered a hard kick to the animal's side, knocking him off the still-frozen Rick. Picking up the rocks that Rick had thrown at the coyote, she threw them back at the creature, who ducked away and slowly retreated.

"Go on!" Kathy hollered at the creature. "Get out of here!" She threw a few more rocks for good measure.

The coyote took off into the growing darkness.

Turning, Kathy saw the panic in her sister's eyes as she indicated Rick on the ground, still posed the same way he had been when the coyote was on top of him.

Unfreezing the scene, Kathy grabbed Rick's hand and helped him up.

On his feet, Rick looked around, disoriented. "What—where did...?" His voice trailed off when his eyes landed on Kathy's face. He cleared his throat and stood up straighter. "Well. We'll need to eat quick. If there's one coyote, then there'll be more."

“Where did it go?” Crystal asked.

“Shh,” Samantha said to distract her. “Here, help me skewer the fish so we can cook it.”

“It’s my fault.” Crystal talked as she followed Samantha’s lead preparing the food. “I’m slowing us down.”

“No, it’s not your fault,” Samantha said. “You warned us. You *saved* us. We just need to move quick to make sure we’re safe.”

Rick knelt down next to Crystal and said, “Don’t worry. Nothing will happen to us as long as Kathy’s around.”

CHAPTER 20

Kathy had been restless. She hadn't been able to sleep out in the cold. After the coyote attack, they hadn't been able to find a covered shelter for the night, so Rick suggested they bury themselves under as many leaves as possible. He reasoned that not only would it provide natural cover for any other predators, but it would keep them warm.

The trouble was, there weren't enough leaves for three of them to sleep under. Not without the proper tools to collect the leaves from around the area like a rake or something.

So Kathy kept waking up because she was cold. Crystal and Samantha were huddled close to each other, sleeping soundly. Kathy was grateful for that. Samantha needed the sleep to help her ankle heal and Crystal sleeping through the night proved that she wasn't nearly as scared as Kathy feared that she was.

Slowly getting up from under the leaves, Kathy found Rick keeping watch from a log several feet away. He huddled into himself in the night cold, but his head was on a swivel.

"You must be freezing," Kathy said quietly as she approached.

He nodded. "I had extra clothes back at the other shelter. Should've grabbed them."

Kathy remembered the clothes he had insisted she and Samantha wear the night before. They had kept them warm through the night. The added layer would've been nice right at that moment too.

She changed the subject to get their minds off of the temperature. "Have you seen anything?"

He shook his head. "No. And that's a good thing. Although I've noticed patterns in the Fishers' hunting behavior."

"Yeah, you said they should've attacked by now," Kathy said. "So now they're acting outside of their behaviors."

"Right. I think you and your sister messed up their plans."

"How so?"

"Usually, they scare their victims out of their cabins and chase them deep into the woods late at night, which pretty much guarantees that they'll still be there in the morning."

Kathy nodded. "Because of the dark and the cold."

"And the wildlife," Rick added. "People are afraid of the dark."

"But people who typically camp? Aren't they used to the wildlife?"

He shrugged. "Used to it, sure. But they're still afraid. Especially if they're chased out without proper weapons. Anyway, once the Fishers get their victims out into the woods, they let them be for the night, letting the anxiety and worry of any potential attack build."

"To scare them."

"Right."

"But that would've been yesterday for me and Samantha and the Fishers never came," Kathy said. "A change in their behavior. And I'm betting you have a theory as to why that changed."

Rick studied the landscape, which was growing clearer to Kathy as her eyes adjusted to the lack of light. "I think they expected you and your sister to be easy targets. Two girls, out on their own. I bet they thought you'd run, get tired, and beg to have your life spared. Then they could hunt you down the next day and kill you like they intended."

Kathy shifted from her perch. The idea of her and her sister dying wasn't an original thought to Kathy, but imagining them being torn apart and mutilated by *humans* was.

"But when they saw you connect up with me, I think they got scared themselves. I've survived for a week out here without them being able to find me. If you two are with me, then there's a greater chance for the two of you to survive as well."

"Too many loose ends for them."

Rick nodded. "Exactly."

"So what do you think their plan is now?"

He sighed. "That's the thing. I don't know. But I'm guessing they're not going to let us go another day without an attack. I think they took yesterday to come up with a new plan to get us. And tomorrow is the day they'll execute it."

"Hopefully the plan is the only thing they're executing."

"Which is why we need to have a plan of our own."

She smirked at him. "I get the feeling that you've already come up with one."

He raised his eyebrows, the hint of a smile lurking on his lips. "Does that bother you?"

"Not at all. At least one of us has some direction around here. Hit me. What are you thinking?"

"We go back to their house first thing in the morning."

She nodded. "Yep. That's our current plan."

"But my guess is, they won't be there. Or, the boys won't be. I'm sure that weird little wife will be there, so we'll have to be careful she doesn't see us. She's a wild card. I haven't had a lot of interaction with her."

"Me neither." Kathy pushed around the few leaves around her feet. She smiled at Rick thinking that the Fishers were weird, just like Kathy and her sister had thought as well.

"I'm willing to bet that somewhere—probably in their barn or something—they have weapons stockpiled. If we can get—"

"What makes you think that?"

"They're hunters."

"Right, and they'll have their weapons *with* them. Especially if they're coming to find us."

Rick hooked an eyebrow. "How many hunters do you know that only have one gun each?"

"How many hunters do I know *period*?" she countered with a devilish grin.

"We own more than one," Rick said. "Not to mention, if Clay and I were staying in the same cabin you and your sister were staying in and it had been wiped out, then we know they at least have mine and Clay's guns."

"How do you know they wouldn't trash them somewhere?"

"And risk us finding them and using them against them?" Rick shook his head. "No. Besides, a hunter throwing out perfectly good guns is like a librarian tossing out perfectly good books. It doesn't make sense."

"Okay. So they're stashing your guns somewhere. That still leaves us short."

"Unless they've chased out other hunters before, which, again, I'm willing to bet they have."

"This sounds like a lot of guessing."

He shrugged. "It's all we've got at this point."

"All right." She let out a breath as she began to recount their new plan. "So they're probably stashing these firearms somewhere. Any idea where?"

Rick rubbed the considerable stubble on his chin. "It'd have to be somewhere away from their main house. They wouldn't want anyone accidentally stumbling on it. If they're clearing out everyone's belongings each time they scare out new victims, the stuff will accumulate pretty quickly. So it'd have to be something large too."

"And probably somewhere on the property," Kathy added. "Within a close enough distance to the house that they could reach it if they need to."

"And get a truck there to drop off the stuff they cleared out from the cabin."

"Which means there'd be a road or a path to it somewhere," Rick finished.

"So the best way to find it is to get close to the main house," Kathy said. "How do you suggest we do that without being spotted by the Fishers, or heard by their dogs? I mean, you have experience hiding, and I'm sure I could pick it up, but my sister has a busted ankle and Crystal is just a kid. And I *don't* want to split up. We're stronger together."

"Agreed." He looked at her and his eyes seemed to bore right into her soul. "I was hoping *you* could help us get through undetected."

"*Me*?" Kathy's heart raced. "What am I supposed to do?"

"I think we both know."

Kathy averted his eyes. They seemed to be able to read every one of her secrets. "I don't think there's anything I can—"

"You've stopped time *at least* twice now that I can tell," he said pointedly. "This last time I *know* I wasn't imagining it. Fess up. What the hell are you?"

There was truly no way out of this. There was no use denying the fact that she was a witch. They needed to stick together if they were going to survive. And then? She'd have to hope that Rick would keep her secret.

The other option was that they weren't going to make it out of the woods alive. And that was a reality she didn't ever want to see come to fruition.

Kathy let out a deep breath to calm her nerves. "I'm a witch."

Rick raised his eyebrows at her confession. "A witch? I have to say, I wasn't expecting that. But it's hard to deny what I saw with my own eyes." He looked off into the darkness. "Okay. So why can't you just snap your fingers and get us out of this mess?"

"It doesn't work like that. My powers are specialized. Focused."

"Limited," he corrected.

She shrugged. "In a way, I guess they are."

"So it's just the time-freezing thing?"

She nodded. "Pretty much."

"Okay." Then, after a few more seconds, "Okay. We can work with that."

"Hold on. You learned my secret, now it's my turn to hear yours. What really happened to Clay? You made us think that he was killed, but you never even *tried* to get revenge for his death?

Or to get out of here yourself? What's keeping you from running? Why have you stuck around for a week?"

Rick turned in on himself again and pulled away from her. "I didn't *see* him die."

"But…?"

"But it's probably what happened to him."

"What do you mean?" Kathy asked. "If you didn't see him die, then there's still a chance that he's alive. Maybe the Fishers are keeping—"

"No!" His voice was stronger than the quiet night warranted. It echoed into the darkness. After a moment, he regained control of himself. "The Fishers don't keep anyone for any reason. Like you said, they don't keep loose ends. He's as good as dead."

With his outburst, Kathy was more determined than ever to get an answer. Especially now that she had told him that she was a witch.

Turning her body toward him, she challenged his hard look with one of her own. "Why don't you tell me what really happened? I think that's only fair."

Rick sighed. "When the Fishers came to chase us out of the cabin, we were completely freaked out. They sent in the dogs—one even took a chunk out of Clay's ass." He smirked, but it quickly soured. "Didn't even have a chance to make fun of him for it."

"What happened?" Kathy reached for his hand and

squeezed it between both of hers. "You can tell me."

Another deep breath. "We made it out of the cabin—somehow. It's all a blur. We must've just bolted out of there. We saw the Fishers on the road and by the creek, which only left the woods to run to. And they were raising their weapons, so we had to move quick."

Flashbacks of Kathy's own similar encounter came to the forefront of her mind. It was something that would never leave her, that feeling of pure panic. Of terror.

"We got to the woods," Rick went on. "We both knew we just needed to run, as fast as we could. Never spoke a word between the two of us, not until Clay tripped." He sucked in another breath and tried to steady his voice, but it wavered. "It was stupid. A damn rock sticking up in the ground. Knocked Clay flat to the ground. I wasn't able to look at it closely, but it ripped his foot up pretty good. He was barefoot. I kept these on." He indicated his boot-covered feet. "Made a big stink about athlete's foot and all that in the cabin. Little did we know it would save my life."

"Couldn't you help him up?"

Rick shook his head. "I offered. I tried to get him to his feet, but Clay pushed me away. Said that he'd only slow me down. We weren't that far into the woods. They had almost caught up to us at that point. Clay was screaming at me to go. I wasn't thinking straight. I just saw them coming—heard the dogs, saw the guns in the Fishers' hands—and I just ran." He buried his head in his hands.

Kathy rubbed his back with one of her hands and clutched his arm with her other. She rested her forehead against his shoulder. She didn't know him well, but she knew he was the type of man who didn't let this side of him be seen often. He was a protector. A thinker. Someone who put his emotions in the backseat time after time.

Now, they were consuming him.

When he picked up his head again, his eyes were wet. "With the dogs coming, I figured the only way they'd lose my scent was to climb a tree. Once I got to the top, I saw the Fishers catch up to Clay. He had dragged himself away from the path we were running on. Tried to bury himself in the leaves, but it didn't work. The damn psychos grabbed his bad led, pulled him out of the leaves, and tied him up like he was already dead." He squeezed his eyes shut and shook his head. "But he was still breathing. Still shouting for them to let him go. Still trying to get away."

Kathy closed her eyes. She couldn't imagine the pain Clay must've gone through. Or the torment that was going on in Rick's mind as he relived the agony of seeing his friend brutalized like that.

"Where did they take him?" Her voice was quiet. Even though she had only known Rick for a little over twenty-four hours, she felt immense sorrow for him. The horrors he would have to face for the rest of his life.

"Last I saw him they were dragging him out of the woods like an animal. I can still hear his voice…" Again, he buried his head in his hands. He rubbed the heels of his hands into his eyes. "He was calling for me. Telling me to run. Find a way to kill the bastards. But I should've done something *then.* I shouldn't have listened to him. I should've saved him."

"No." Kathy set her hands on his shoulders and turned him to face her. "No! Rick, you did what he asked. You ran, like he told you to do. If you hadn't listened, then it would've been four against one. They would've killed you. And then who would've been around to save me and Samantha, like you did last night? Or Crystal?"

Rick pulled away from her and stood. "You don't understand. I can't get the sound of his voice out of my head. Calling to me. Telling me to run. And then, a few hours later, I *swore* I heard his screams."

Kathy wasn't even going to entertain the idea that Clay was alive. She knew as well as Rick did that the Fishers had probably killed him right away. No loose ends.

But she still wanted to provide Rick with comfort. With closure. Otherwise, he'd be carrying this burden for the rest of his life.

"Rick, come sit down." She patted the log next to her. "We can talk about it. I'm sure—"

"There's nothing we can do now," Rick said. "He's dead."

"Rick…"

"I'm going to bed. If your sister isn't up in two hours, you'll need to wake her up."

Kathy's shoulders slumped as she watched him walk off to their makeshift leaf bed. Somehow, at the moment, Rick's future scared her more than anything else.

CHAPTER 21

Their day had started early. At the very first sign of daybreak, Samantha had woken the rest of them up after her watch and they began marching through the woods.

The first stop was the creek bed again, where Rick spent the next half hour hunting for their daily fish breakfast. While he hunted, the girls started a fire right at the creek bed. They were taking the Fishers head-on today. Either they were going home or they were going to the afterlife. Hiding traces of their whereabouts was less concerning than taking the Fishers by surprise.

After they ate, they started back toward the Fisher homestead. None of them spoke. The new plan that Rick and Kathy had discussed the night before had been explained over breakfast. Now, as they hiked, the four of them were silent as their minds raced with worry.

"What's that?" Crystal pointed at something in the trees.

The other three stopped and looked.

"What's what?" Rick asked.

"I see it," Samantha said. "It looks like..."

"A barn," Kathy finished. She turned to Rick. "Do you think this could be the one we're looking for?"

Rick stepped forward to get a better view, then turned in the direction they had been moving in. "But the Fisher house has to be several miles that way."

"You said their storage barn would have to be somewhere hidden." Kathy gestured to the barn. "*This* is hidden."

"It's worth checking out," Samantha offered. "There might be things in there that we can use. Something that's stronger than these homemade weapons we have."

Rick nodded. "Okay. But we need to move quietly. We don't know if the Fishers are there now."

Although the day was gloomy, the full strength of the daylight was out, eliminating any advantage they had with their early start to the day. There were no shadows to hide in anymore.

Rick led the way. Samantha walked closely behind Crystal, keeping her hands on the girl's shoulders as they walked. Kathy kept her eyes peeled for any unexpected visitors lurking in the trees.

There was a small clearing around the barn. When they came around the front, they saw tire tracks matting the grass down, but no other signs of life.

Kathy pointed to the tracks, which led into the brush. "Hidden path for a truck."

"Have you seen this barn before in your tour throughout the property?" Samantha asked Rick.

He shook his head. "No. Then again, I've tried to stay *away* from the Fisher house as much as possible."

"Are the bad men in there?" Crystal asked quietly.

None of the adults could provide her with an honest answer, so her question hung in the air.

"You three stay out here while I go check it out," Rick said.

"No, you're going to need protection," Kathy said. "I'm coming too."

Samantha looked to the side of the barn. "Crystal and I will be waiting on the other side, in case someone pulls up."

They split up. Rick waited until Samantha and Crystal were safely out of sight to slide open the large barn door.

Inside smelled musty and stale, but it was otherwise empty. Kathy pulled the doors open as wide as they could to let in the light.

"What is all of this?" she asked.

There were piles of *things* on the floor. Bags, clothing, coolers, grills, shoes, lawn chairs, and, stacked along the far wall, a collection of guns and other weapons.

"I think this is what we were talking about last night," Rick said. "This is where they put all of the stuff they clean out of the cabins after they scare off their victims."

"But it's a long way from the cabin."

He nodded. "It has to be, so nobody accidentally finds it. Why do you think they spent the time putting in all of those trails? They don't want you aimlessly wandering through the woods and discovering their secrets."

Kathy walked among the rows of collected—*stolen*—items. "They must've been planning this for *years*."

"Something like this I don't think was planned," he said. "I think it is what they slowly evolved to, though."

"Either way, it's sick."

Rick crouched down. "Here's my bag. Still has all of my clothes in it." He pulled it out and tossed it toward the door. "If you find yours, we can bring that with us too."

"I'm more concerned about getting out of here than finding my stuff," Kathy mumbled as she looked around. Some of the items clearly belonged to children. Pink lawn chairs, tiny motorized ATVs, even little bikes. Her thoughts went to Josh and her stomach turned with the idea of someone harming an innocent child.

Rick went to the wall with the firearms and started picking through for his own weapons. "Samantha was right. We can all be armed with these. Now we just need to find the right ammunition for each of these."

At the end of the row Kathy was looking at, she saw a door leading into a small room sectioned out in the corner of the barn. Slowly, she pushed open the door and froze when she saw what was inside.

"What's in there?" Rick asked from behind her.

She opened her mouth to respond, but nothing came out. How could she put this into words?

Rick came up next to her and peered in for himself. "Their souvenirs."

The room was lined with shelves, all of which held skulls, femurs, and other bones of varying sizes. Among them was jewelry and other knickknacks taken from their victims.

"This is sick." Kathy's mouth turned down in disgust.

"Then you're probably not going to want to go downstairs." Rick pointed to the small staircase tucked in the corner under the shelves.

She looked up at him. "I feel like we should. Just in case there's someone down there, hiding out and afraid."

He raised his eyebrows and looked around. "You think they'd stay here? After passing through the room of *bones*?"

She shrugged. "People do crazy things when they're desperate. Look at us. We're willing to go *down* there."

Rick smirked. "Good point." Without another word, he led her down the creaky staircase.

The basement was dimly-lit. The only natural light came from the holes in the foundation and the floorboards above their heads. And yet, it was fairly tall. The dirt floor allowed enough head room for them to stand comfortably in.

Kathy made another face as the stench of decay hit her. "Ugh, what is that *smell*?"

Rick pointed to the ground. Most of the dirt had been soaked in dried blood.

"What's that fro—" She never had a chance to finish her sentence. The suddenly shift in Rick's behavior stopped her in her tracks. Something was off. Something she hadn't seen yet. She was afraid to find out what that something was. "What?"

He never answered. Instead, he turned and escaped up the stairs.

Kathy was tempted to follow him. The idea of being alone in a creepy basement filled with blood in a barn in the middle of the woods turned her stomach upside down. But there was *something* that Rick had seen that had set him off.

Her eyes scanned the room. While the blood on the dirt floor was terrible and sad, it wasn't the worst that she'd ever seen. What was it that had struck him like that?

Then she saw it.

Stacked on the rotting wooden work bench tucked in the corner was the head of a young man. And based on Rick's reaction, she was willing to bet that it was Clay.

CHAPTER 22

Kathy raced up the stairs to find Rick. Based on what they had seen in the basement, she knew that he wasn't thinking rationally. And, from what little she knew about him, she knew he would resist all the proper emotions of finding his best friend's severed head and channel it into a blinding rage.

Kathy was not about to watch him die. Not by doing something stupid.

Upstairs, she found him stuffing items from the collected weapons into a duffel bag that he had snatched up from another pile.

"Rick, what are you going to do?" She walked right up to him and put a hand on his arm, hoping that a physical touch would help break him out of whatever psychological avoidance he was locked into.

"I'm going to do what needs to be done."

"And what exactly does that mean?" She ducked under his arm as it reached out for another rifle, and got between him and the collection of weapons.

"They're going to pay for what they did," he said. "What they're doing to all of us." He stepped around her to look at the weapons lined up further down the wall.

"Okay, but you have to think logically here," she said. "Now is not the time to go in guns-a-blazing. *Literally*. We have a plan."

"We *had* a plan to escape and stop the Fishers. Now, I want them dead, and I don't want any of you implicated, so I need to do this alone."

Apparently he *had* thought this out.

"You want to get justice for Clay. I get that. But do you really think you can take on four of them all by yourself? That's suicide. You have to think rationally."

He turned on her with a mean look. "All rationality went out the window when they forced us out of our cabin."

Kathy froze at being snapped at. She could almost feel the raw, barely controlled rage radiating off him.

Rick turned back to his work. Buried at the bottom of the pile were explosives, which he added to the bag.

"Come on," Kathy pleaded. "You have to let us help. If we

keep going with the plan that you and I came up with last night, we can stop the Fishers. There's no way they won't be prosecuted. They'll spend the rest of their lives in prison. Possibly even death row!"

He shook his head. "It's not good enough. Clay didn't die for maybes and possiblys."

"If you kill them, there's a good chance *you'll* be sitting in prison instead."

He turned on her. "Do you know what they were saying when they tied him up like an animal and dragged him away like he was nothing but trash?"

Kathy licked her lips and swallowed. It was all she could do to not crumble to his intense glare. "No."

"They were *laughing*. Called him *boy*. Joked about how he wasn't fast enough." Rick shook his head. "This is all a game to them, and I'm done playing. It's time *we* start making up the rules."

With his bag filled, Rick zipped it up and slung it over his shoulder. The contents rattled inside and the straps pulled tightly from the weight. He started toward the door.

"I can stop you, you know," Kathy called to him. "If I really wanted to, I could keep freezing you until it's too late for you to do anything."

In the light of the doorway, he turned and looked back at her. "Well, I guess I can't stop you from doing that. But then I'd need to make a choice of my own."

Her heart beat a little faster. Was that a threat? "What do you mean by that?"

Rick readjusted the strap on his shoulder and gave her a sad look. Another moment later, he turned and left the barn. Kathy worried that that was the last time she'd ever see him alive again, so she ran to the door and watched as he made his way down the overgrown path.

She wanted to call out to him. To tell him to stay. To go with him to protect him. But even though she understood it, she didn't believe in his mission for vengeance. And she couldn't leave her injured sister and little Crystal behind.

Samantha peered around the corner of the barn and, upon seeing it was safe, she and Crystal came to stand next to Kathy.

"Where's he going?" Samantha asked. "And where did he get the guns sticking out of his bag?"

Kathy kept her eyes on the spot in the trees where she had last seen Rick. She shook her head. "We need to follow him. Make sure he's not going to do something stupid and get in over his head. Because that's exactly what's going to happen if he goes out alone."

"But why?" Samantha turned back to the barn. "What exactly did you find in there?"

Kathy finally pulled her eyes away and looked down at Crystal, then met her sister's eyes. "We found Clay. Or rather, we found part of him."

CHAPTER 23

- 1985 -

It took a while, but Jim and Donovan finally met up with Pete and Kurt. They each carried more weapons than necessary, but that allowed Jim and Donovan to restock their own supplies.

"You two ready to go hunting?" Jim asked.

Pete nodded. "We tried to push the critter in your direction, but we lost sight of it."

"That's good, son." Jim put a hand on his shoulder. "We'll find it. There's four of us now. We'll have to work together."

"What critter are we hunting?" Kurt asked.

"It's a dangerous one," Jim said. "Unlike anything else we've had to hunt before."

Donovan stared at the ground. "My father."

Pete and Kurt didn't say anything as they looked between Jim and Donovan.

"We can't hunt Uncle Rodney," Kurt started. "He's—"

Jim shook his head. "He's not your uncle anymore. In fact, he's not even human. He's our prey."

"Is that who…?" Pete looked at Donovan and touched his own face, finishing the sentence with his actions.

Donovan simply nodded.

"All right, you look here," Jim said, addressing his sons. "You may not agree with me, but trust me when I say that there are reasons we're hunting Rodney. He—*It*—crossed a line. Now, this isn't our normal hunting trip. I get that. But when I say we're going to hunt Rodney, then that's what we're going to do. Understood?"

Pete and Kurt both nodded. Pete chanced a look in Donovan's direction.

Donovan saw the sympathetic look in his cousin's eyes and he balled his fists at the thought of appearing so weak. "I want the kill shot."

Pete and Kurt both looked stunned, although neither of them said anything.

Jim put a hand on Donovan's shoulder. "You've earned it, son." He nodded back into the thicket of the woods. "Let's move out, boys."

Wordlessly, the four of them fell into their hunting patterns. They each held their weapons at the ready, stepping through the undergrowth carefully to make as little noise as possible. They kept their eyes and ears open, scanning back and forth, looking and listening for sounds of movement. Each of them twenty-five or thirty feet apart from one another, casting a wide net through the woods as they moved.

Every now and then, they would nod to each other or gesture with their hands to indicate that they spotted tracks or some other indication that their prey—Rodney—had traveled in their direction.

The going was slow. Each of them were tired of being on high alert for so long. Even Donovan was beginning to question the rationale behind hunting his father down. But Uncle Jim had already killed his mother. They needed to finish the hunt properly.

"Oh, God no!"

The voice carried through the woods. Familiar. This was near where Donovan's mother had been executed.

Jim motioned for the four of them to circle the clearing where Gretchen's body lay and the boys moved into action.

Kneeling beside the body, Rodney stared down at his dead wife.

"You stupid bitch," he said. "You could never run for shit. Even to save your damn life."

Donovan heard a twig crack under his foot and saw his father's head tilt to the side at the sound. Slowly, then frantically, Rodney looked around.

"Who's there?" His voice sounded more confident than he probably was. That thought made Donovan smile.

Donovan couldn't spot his uncle for confirmation, but his hunting instincts told him now that he'd been found out, there was no sense in keeping up pretenses. He rose and stepped into the clearing.

Very shortly after, Kurt, Pete, and, later, Jim, each stepped into the clearing one-by-one.

Rodney smiled at the sight of his son. "Donnie. My boy. What are we doing here? This is crazy. You don't want to hurt me. Whatever this is that you're feeling toward me, don't let it turn you into something that you're going to regret. We can work things out. Come to an understanding."

Donovan raised his gun in the direction of his father. "I understand things perfectly."

Rodney laughed. "What are you going to do? Shoot me? You're just a little boy. You don't have the guts."

"Don't push him, Rod," Jim warned. "You've done nothing but underestimate him his whole life."

"Underestimate him? What am I missing? The poor schmuck is nothing but a disappointment. He's twenty years old and has no job, no girlfriend, no sense of drive at all. He hasn't accomplished a single thing in his life." He looked Donovan right in the eyes. "You're pathetic. And a waste of my time."

Donovan began to lower his weapon.

"See! You can't even bring yourself to shoot someone when

they're taunting you. Do you even know that I'm picking on you? Or are you too stupid to—"

The gun fired and Rodney fell to the ground with a roar of pain.

"You bastard!" He clutched at his knee, which was a deep crimson as blood poured out of it.

Donovan approached his father, gun raised to shoot him. Then he saw an opportunity and took it.

He grasped his father's leg—the lower half of the one he had shot—and yanked on it.

"Ah!" Rodney cried out.

Donovan twisted, loving the sound of his father in pain. *Now* who was the pathetic one? After the way Rodney had beat on Donovan so easily back in the trailer, it was nice to finally be in a position of power for once.

Rodney swung his good leg around and it connected with the side of Donovan's face. Hard.

He dropped Rodney's bad leg and fell to the ground.

"Hey!" Pete rushed to his cousin's aid, brandishing his knife and began swinging it at Rodney, who put up his arms to protect himself.

With the new blood that poured from the slashes on Rodney's arms, Pete was making pretty good work of his knife. Rodney retracted his foot, but before a warning could be sounded off by one of the onlookers, Rodney drove his heel straight into Pete's chest and sent him flying backwards.

Even while gasping for breath, Pete stood and hurled his knife in Rodney's direction, but it soared right past his head.

"Don't you ever throw your weapon away like that!" Jim hollered as he rushed up to assist.

Rodney smirked and looked at Pete. "Better listen to your *daddy*, boy!"

This time, Kurt stepped up and raised his own rifle and pointed it at Rodney's crotch. "I'll shoot the damn thing off and we'll see who's calling who *boy*."

Rodney shrugged. "So shoot. I'm as good as dead anyway." He turned to look at Donovan. "You see? Your kid cousin even has to clean up your messes for you because you don't have the balls to do it." Then he looked to Jim. "Are you happy now? You've turned my boy against me, just like you've always wanted."

Jim shook his head. "No, Rod. You did that to yourself. All I'm doing is teaching your son how to stand up for himself."

Donovan retrieved his gun from the ground and then stood. He stepped to his father and pressed his boot on his father's foot. He put pressure on it, causing it to pull at his injured knee. With his hands, he raised the rifle and held it against Rodney's forehead.

Despite his best efforts, his hands shook. His body knew he was at a turning point in his life. He was about to cross a line that could never be undone.

"You're not going to shoot me," Rodney said. "You don't

have the guts. Just look at you. Shaking like a leaf. You're *weak*, Donnie. You always have been and you always will be!" He smiled, even as the rifle pressed against his forehead.

"What do you know about strength?" Donovan asked. Before an answer could come, he fired the gun.

Rodney's head exploded with a spray of red that covered the front of Donovan, all over Gretchen's body, and the earth around them.

As the gunshot echoed into the woods, the remaining four looked on quietly.

Jim was the first to break the silence. "You did good, son." He put a hand on Donovan's shoulder. Then, he turned to the other boys. "Now, we need to take care of the bodies."

Kurt cleared his throat and turned away from the carnage. "What are we going to do with them?"

Jim looked at the blood splatter that had been his brother, then turned back to his son. "Well. Your mother said we need to restock the freezer. And we *did* just go hunting."

CHAPTER 24

Samantha, Kathy, and Crystal worked their way back to the main house in a roundabout way. Samantha led the way, making sure to keep a safe distance from Rick by tapping into his thoughts with her telepathic abilities. He was in no shape to listen to reason at the moment, and no matter how much Kathy tried to convince him to not face off against the Fishers alone, she knew he was going to try to do it anyway.

The best thing they could do was keep an eye on him for now.

Finally, the girls came on the main house minutes after Rick had arrived. The first thing they heard were the dogs barking. Upon closer inspection, it sounded as if it were coming from the barn on the other side of the driveway.

Rick wasted no time and got right to work. Sneaking along the back of the house, he began to pull things from his duffel bag. He started at one corner of the house, moved further down the outer wall and sat there for a moment with his back to the girls before moving on down the wall again and repeating the same thing.

Kathy couldn't quite make out what he was doing from their far-away vantage point. "What's going on?"

"He's planting explosives around the house," Samantha murmured. Her eyes remained closed as she tapped into his thoughts. Suddenly, her words struck her and her eyes snapped open. "You guys found *explosives* in that barn?"

"Shh!" Kathy waved her away and squinted, trying to focus on Rick. He had moved around the corner of the house and out of her sight.

"He's an idiot," Samantha muttered as she watched.

"At least he's not just running in like an idiot," Kathy commented. "He seems to have *some* semblance of a plan. I was afraid that he was going to throw caution to the wind and go in there willy-nilly." She wondered if her warnings before he left had sunk in to his brain on his way to the main house. Even if it was a subconscious admission that she was right, if it kept him alive and well, that's all that truly mattered.

"Well, that's all fine and good, as long as he doesn't get caught." Samantha nodded to the pile of junkers sitting in the weeds. "Found my car. All the rest of those cars must belong to other victims too."

"I bet none of them work," Kathy said. "Not if they cut one of the lines in yours when they first scared us out of the cabin."

"Too bad. Otherwise that could've been our getaway."

"Are they home?" Crystal asked.

"Rick doesn't seem to think so," Kathy said.

Crystal pointed to the driveway. "But their truck is still here."

The sisters peeled their eyes away to see for themselves. Kathy's heart sank.

"They're in the house," Samantha said. "I definitely saw a man move around inside through the window."

"So much for Rick's theory that they go out hunting on the third day," Kathy muttered. "We have to help him."

"How?" Samantha asked. "If we go down there, it could draw attention to *us* and then the Fishers will come out and attack all of us. We're not ready for that."

Kathy wondered if they were ever going to be ready for it. "But we have to do something."

"Kathy, if you go down there, you could be sending Rick right to the grave."

Crystal began to whimper quietly to herself.

Samantha reached for the girl to comfort her but stopped when something at the main house caught her eye.

The door swung open and out walked Jim, followed by one of his sons, Pete.

And Rick was taking a chance and sprinting toward the barn on the opposite edge of the driveway with his duffel bouncing on his back.

"They see him," Kathy murmured. "They're going to shoot—"

"They're not going to shoot that close to the house, Kathy."

"They're *hunting* us for *sport*, Sam. They have no scruples."

Samantha was quiet as she watched. Her sister had a point. All rules and laws had been thrown out the window in this nightmare.

"Hey!" Jim called to Rick.

The barking from the dogs seemed to increase in intensity.

"We have a runner!" Pete shouted back into the house. "Grab the guns!"

Donovan and Kurt each raced out of the house, hollering with adrenaline and laughter, and carrying weapons and tossing extras in the direction of Jim and Pete. Kathy thought they resembled hyenas, manic with their overwhelming emotions.

Rick hesitated as he saw the Fishers come out of the house and it wasn't long before they had circled around him. The predators closing in on their prey. The dogs, somehow sensing the tension, were hollering wildly from inside the barn.

Turning slowly in circles to cover all positions, Rick pulled a grenade out of the bag and held it above his head. "Don't shoot! Don't shoot or I'll blow everything up!"

Kathy started to stand, ready to race to his aid, but Samantha pulled her back.

"Don't you *dare*," she hissed.

"What are you going to do?" Jim asked Rick. "How do you expect to throw that grenade if you're dead?"

"I don't need to be alive to blow it up," Rick said.

The boys all looked at each other, but Jim kept his eyes on Rick.

"So what?" Jim shrugged. "Is this supposed to be the part where I apologize for all of my wrongdoings and you convince me to change my ways?"

"There's no changing you," Rick said. "You're too far gone."

"Then what do you want? Why not just blow us up?"

Kathy slowly sunk back down from where she stood. Something had been bothering her too. Why had Rick decided to run out to the barn across the driveway when it was so open? Obviously he would've been spotted there. Why not skirt around the edges to plant the explosives around the perimeter of the barn like he had done with the house?

Because he wanted to be caught.

"I want to know why," Rick said. "Why are you doing this?"

"Doing what? Hunting?" Jim smirked. "Because it's fun! And listening to the cries of the powerless as we show them just how powerful *we* are gives a certain thrill that money can't buy." Again, he sneered. "And your little friend was *begging* me at the end to spare his life."

Rick raised his other hand up and reached for the pin.

Kathy shot to her feet and started through the brush before Samantha could grab her again. She needed to get to Rick. She needed to save him. She needed to freeze the scene and use her magic to *protect* him instead of *harm* the Fishers.

She just needed to do something.

"Damn it, Kathy," Samantha murmured from her post in the weeds. She began to stand to follow, but Crystal tugged at her arm hard. "You have to be brave, sweetie. Find somewhere to hide. Run back to the shelter we stayed at and—"

"No!" The girl's screams carried across the openness.

Samantha sunk down lower to cover their position. "What is it? What's the matter?"

The girl's face was a mess with tears and snot. Samantha couldn't help but console her.

"Don't go," the girl pleaded. "My mom and dad told me they'd come back for me and they never did. Don't go! Don't leave me." She wrapped her arms around Samantha and clung to her.

The witch melted, falling back onto the moist ground and pulling Crystal in for a tight embrace. How could she leave this poor defenseless *scared* girl?

But then her eyes snapped open and she saw Kathy running directly at the monsters who caused all of this. Suddenly, Samantha wanted to split herself in two and protect them both.

CHAPTER 25

"Stop!" Kathy's voice carried across the open space of the driveway as she barreled through the brush. "Don't touch him!"

The four Fishers all turned their attention to her as she ran into view. As she approached, she saw that Rick had time to pull out a handgun from his bag. Stepping behind Pete, who stood closest to him, Rick wrapped his arm around his captive and pointed the gun at his head. Pete struggled, but Rick's grip was firm.

"Drop the gun!" he demanded of Pete.

The Fisher looked to his father for approval.

Jim nodded. "Do what he says, son."

Rick waved his gun in the direction of the other Fishers.

"Now drop your guns!"

Nobody moved. Everyone stared at him. In the barn, the dogs barked on.

"I'll shoot him!" Rick threatened, pointing the gun back to Pete's head.

Still, nobody moved.

"So what's your plan?" Jim asked. "You shoot him and you think the rest of us will crumble with sadness and turn a blind eye to the two of you escaping? You think we aren't numb to death?" He laughed. "We're the ones who *started* all of this! Death is what we do!"

Beyond him, Kathy saw Pete stand rigid at the end of Rick's weapon. He swallowed hard, but kept his face expressionless.

"No, you're going to chase me," Kathy called out. "That's what you want, isn't it? The thrill of the hunt? That's how you sickos get your jollies."

Kurt licked his lips and rubbed his hands together. "Oh, I've got some ideas for you, sweetheart. Some *special* ideas that we'll both love." He started marching toward her. "You asked, so here I come."

"Keep it in your pants, Kurt," Donovan said from behind his cousin.

But Kurt didn't listen. He continued his even pace toward Kathy, who took a careful step backward. There was something about the look in his eye that turned her stomach more than the other Fishers' own murderous gazes. The hunger she saw in

Kurt's eyes was somehow more predatory than the others.

Rick shifted the aim of his gun to Kurt. "Take another step and you die."

"Rick, don't—" Kathy started to call to him, but she saw Pete spin around and quickly wrap a rope around Rick's neck.

In another second, Jim was on top of Rick. He pulled his gun from his hand and kicked him in the leg, dropping him to the ground with a grunt of pain while Pete yanked on the rope from behind Rick.

Kathy put up her hands and froze the scene. She might not have been able to overpower the Fishers or out-arm them, but she could at least stop them in their tracks.

She ran up to Jim and pulled Rick's gun from his grip. She raised it to Jim Fisher's back, frozen by her magic, and tried to will herself to squeeze the trigger, but she couldn't. Killing him wouldn't make her any better than them. Especially not in these unfair circumstances. She wanted him to be punished, but she wasn't sure she could dole out the punishment herself.

But she could try to save Rick.

Hurling the gun into the weeds, Kathy turned her attention on the rope, which was pulled tightly around Rick's neck, held in place by Pete, who stood behind him.

Kathy tried to carefully lace her fingers between the rope and Rick's neck, but it was too tight. She considered unfreezing just Rick, but if she couldn't get the rope loosened, he would suffocate anyway.

There was only one thing she could do.

Taking a step back, she wound up and delivered a hard kick into Pete's stomach, which knocked him to the gravel driveway, rope in hand.

Consequently, the other Fishers unfroze and she was suddenly in the center of them all.

Driving an elbow into Jim's side, Kathy started toward the woods in a direction opposite where Samantha and Crystal lay in hiding. The last thing she wanted to do was expose them.

But before she could break from the group, Donovan grabbed her arm and yanked her back. She struggled as he fell on top of her and pinned her arms to the ground.

"You bitch! How the hell did you move so fast?" he asked.

Kathy gritted her teeth. She brought her knee up hard and jammed it right into his groin.

His strength left him and he crumpled to the ground.

Kathy pushed him off and then shot to her feet as Kurt and Jim turned on her. Pete had regained his stance and wrapped the rope around Rick's throat again.

"You want to die with your little boyfriend, pretty girl?" Jim asked. "I think my boy would like a few rounds with you first. Should I let your boyfriend watch?"

She raised her arms to freeze again, but Kurt was suddenly beside her. She moved just in time to avoid his attempt to snatch her.

Backpedaling fast, she saw Pete tie off the rope at Rick's

throat before moving to tie his hands with the other end of the rope. At least his face wasn't blue anymore. And if Jim wanted to truly torture Rick by forcing him to watch Kurt violate her, then that meant they would keep him alive until they caught her.

Turning, she darted into the woods. Branches smacked her face and the rustle of leaves did nothing to hide her whereabouts.

It didn't matter, though. Kurt was hot on her trail.

If there was any hope of saving Rick, she needed to run. She couldn't get caught.

CHAPTER 26

Kathy's heart pounded in her chest as she raced through the woods. She jumped over fallen logs, ducked under branches, and avoided puddles and muddy spots as much as possible. Behind her, she heard the footsteps of Kurt close by. But what scared her more was the sound of the dogs snarling and barking right on his tail.

In her head she kept replaying what Rick had told her about Clay—how he had tripped over a rock and scraped up his bare foot when the Fishers had chased him and Rick out of their cabin. And then the Fishers grabbed him and later decapitated him.

No, Kathy thought to herself. *That's not going to happen to you. Focus. Get away.*

She was by no means an expert on the layout of the Fisher property, but she knew enough to avoid the barn with all the supplies—for all she knew Samantha and Crystal were back there waiting for her—and the cabins strung along the pothole-filled dirt road—which Kathy now believed to be an intentional way to slow down anyone who might try to escape if they managed to get access to a vehicle.

The shelter that Rick had dug out was on the other side of the creek across the ravine, so she didn't have to worry about accidentally exposing that. Then again, if she came up on the ravine, where would she go? Where would she hide? And how would she stop the dogs from tracking her down?

She needed a plan.

The sound of her pursuers running behind her scared her. Kurt thrashed through the fallen leaves, smushed through mud, and used the fallen logs as objects to propel himself forward. He didn't share her concerns about the environment around him. Meanwhile, the dogs were faster than her, quickly gaining on her as she ran for her life.

Kathy, however, was growing tired. Apparently Kurt wasn't. Or not as quickly as she was.

Get down.

Samantha's voice popped into her head so quickly that Kathy barely had time to decide whether to listen to it or not. Her witch sense told her to trust her instincts and she dove into the pile of leaves ahead of her.

"Ah!" Kurt groaned behind her as she heard branches snapping against one another.

The dogs weren't bothered by the swinging branch. One jumped on Crystal while the other jumped on Samantha.

Kathy shot to her feet and quickly put up her hands and froze everything. The dog on top of Crystal had its teeth set on her throat, but there was no blood. Kathy had stopped him in time.

She turned to her sister and saw her crawling out from under the dog who had pinned her, now magically frozen in time.

"You okay?" Samantha asked her sister.

"Yeah," Kathy said breathlessly. "You?"

"I'm tired of this shit." For someone who never usually swore, her statement was very telling.

Samantha searched the forest floor and found Kurt's gun, which had skidded several feet away from him when he fell.

"What are we going to do?" Kathy asked. "Shoot him?"

Samantha seemed to consider it, then said, "I don't know if I could do that. Especially not like this, with him frozen."

"I know, but, Sam…" Kathy pointed to the dog about to tear into Crystal's throat.

"Oh, no you don't!" Samantha delivered a hard kick to the dog, which broke him out of Kathy's magic and sent him flying into the leaves off of Crystal.

The girl shot to her feet and rushed to Kathy's side. "What's going on?"

"Just stay behind me," Kathy warned.

The dog quickly got back to its feet and squared off with Samantha. He bared his teeth and snarled, but Samantha refused to back down. Then, he lunged.

Samantha raised the gun and fired, causing the dog to squirm and fall to the ground as it bled out.

Crystal shrieked from Kathy's side. "Is he dead?"

"If he's not, he will be," Kathy told her as she watched the dog take its last few breaths. As heartless as it felt, she had no remorse for the dog's passing. "What about the other two?" Kathy indicated the other frozen dog and Kurt.

She still hadn't been able to catch her breath. Now, even with her sense of relief, she found it hard to take big enough gulps of air as the fear of what she had just been through sank in.

Samantha studied her sister, then extended her free arm. "Come here."

Kathy closed the distance and embraced her sister in a tight sideways hug. It felt good to have some comfort in all of the madness. And there was no doubt about it, Kathy felt calmer because of it.

"I'm glad you're safe," Samantha said by Kathy's ear. "Even if you did an incredibly *stupid* thing."

"But it worked." The younger sister offered a smirk as she pulled away. "Rick wasn't killed."

"Yeah, but after you left he's not in good shape, either," Samantha said. "Are you good?"

Kathy nodded. The reminder that Rick was still hogtied by those psychos sobered her. She absently wrapped a protective arm around Crystal, who clung to her for her own comfort.

"Good," Samantha said. "Crystal, get behind us."

The little girl complied without question.

"If we're going to save Rick, we need to move fast," Samantha told her sister.

Kathy closed her eyes as she breathed in a deep breath of air. She let it out slowly, then opened her eyes. "Ready."

Samantha nodded, then Kathy unfroze Kurt.

"Don't move," Samantha warned him.

"You don't tell me what to do." He turned on his back so he could face them. "I'll have my way with all three of you."

Samantha turned the gun on the frozen dog. "Take a look at your companion. One down, the other one stopped in his tracks. Do you really want to test us?"

"How did you…what did you do to him?"

"The same thing we'll do to you if you don't listen," Kathy said. "Now, let's go."

Kurt rolled, as if he were going to get up, but lunged toward his dog instead, which broke Kathy's magic. The dog snarled as it resumed its attack on Samantha, who was no longer beneath him. Quickly recovering, the dog turned and rushed toward the girls.

Without a moment's hesitation, Samantha raised the gun and fired. The first shot missed, the second nicked the dog's rear leg, but the third shot was a head shot and dropped the dog instantly.

"Dale!" Kurt cried out. "You shot my dog, you stupid bitch!"

"And I'll shoot you too if you don't cooperate," Samantha warned. "Now *get up*!"

With a look full of pure hatred, Kurt rose to his feet.

"You're our prisoner now," Kathy told him. "And you're going to help us save our friend."

CHAPTER 27

"It's just for a little while, sweetie," Samantha said as Crystal clung to her. "I promise you, we'll be back." She let her persuasion power lace her words, trying to soothe the young girl's worried mind, but even magic wasn't enough to fix the trauma Crystal had been through.

"No, I don't want you to disappear like my mommy!" Crystal whined.

"Honey, where we're going isn't safe. But it's something we need to do in order for us to go home." She shook her head. "We don't want you to get hurt. We need you to stay far away from the house."

Crystal looked down at the ground, her face still turned down in a frown. "I'm scared."

Samantha squeezed the girl's hands. She hated that there wasn't more she could do to comfort her. "I know you are. But I need you to be brave. Can you do that for me?"

"I can try." Her voice was small, almost inaudible, but Samantha heard it all the same.

"Good. Now, I need you to go up to the second story of the barn and hide out in the loft. And don't come out until you hear me or Kathy call out the password, okay?"

Crystal nodded, then turned back to the barn.

They had marched Kurt over to the barn where they had found all the stolen items from previous guests. The gun was pointed at his back the whole time because they had nothing to restrain his hands with. Now, at the barn, they had supplies to rummage through to get the ropes that they needed to bind him. And while Kathy used her magic to freeze then bind their prisoner, Samantha was trying to convince a terrified eight-year-old that she'd be safe, when Samantha didn't even believe the words herself.

"We'll come back for you," the older witch promised, hating how hollow the words sounded.

She led Crystal inside and stood at the bottom of the ladder that led up to the loft while Crystal climbed up. There was no telling what animals had nested up there but, all thing's considered, this was still the best hiding spot around.

"We'll come back for you," Samantha repeated. "Stay out of sight and stay quiet until you hear the password. We'll be as quick as we can."

Crystal popped her little head over the side of the half wall and nodded before ducking back down.

Samantha left the barn and closed the doors behind her. She pressed her back against the closed doors and hoped that she could come through for Crystal.

"Ready?" Kathy asked from a few feet away. She held the gun at Kurt's back.

He looked smug. Like this was all some simple game. As if lives hadn't been lost—and more still in danger—from the actions of his family.

"Yeah." Samantha started down the overgrown path. "Let's get this over with."

The three of them were silent as they followed the path back to the main house. As they got closer, the girls made Kurt walk in front of them in case there was a surprise attack. But, Samantha figured that the Fishers would be satisfied now that they had Rick to toy with for a little while. Especially since he had evaded them for so long.

She just hoped they weren't torturing him. Or more realistically, that they weren't hurting him *too* bad. The torture was a given with these people.

Across the driveway, Donovan stepped into the doorway of the barn. When he saw them approach, he pulled his gun from the waistline of his pants behind him and pointed it at them.

"You've got to be real stupid to come back here," he said.

"Don't shoot," Samantha commanded. She continued to

march on until they all stood in the middle of the large driveway. "We want to make a trade."

"Uncle Jim!" Donovan kept his eyes—and his gun—on the girls as he called back into the barn. "Come out here!"

Jim came walking out while he wiped his hands in a rag. Samantha could see that it was bloody.

Rick's blood.

"They're hurting him," Kathy grumbled from beside her sister.

Quiet, Samantha pushed into her mind.

"We're offering a trade," Samantha said again. "Your son for our friend."

"Assuming he's even alive," Kathy added.

Jim smirked and, as if on cue, Rick's screams sounded from inside the barn. "My boy Pete is still, uh, *working* on him. But yes, he's very much alive. Can't say for how much longer, but we'll see how he holds out." He looked to Donovan. "What did you bet? Two days of this torture? I, myself, think he's good for at least three, maybe even four days."

Revulsion nearly overpowered Samantha, but she forced it away. These people were soulless. They didn't care that they were inflicting immense amounts of pain for their *entertainment*.

"Enough games!" Kathy shouted. "Let him go and we'll give you Kurt back."

Shut up! Samantha telepathically transmitted to her sister.

You're ruining the deal by sounding too desperate! He's toying with us.

They're killing him, Sam, Kathy quietly shot back.

Jim just shook his head. "I raised my kids to be smarter than this. Never chase down prey. They're better hunters than that." He shrugged. "Or so I thought. Kurt, son, if you were dumb enough to forget what I'd taught you, you deserve to pay the consequences."

"Do we have a deal or not?" Samantha demanded.

Gritting his teeth and forcing a smile, Jim said, "My son is a grown man. He made a mistake while hunting. Now he needs to pay the price." He reached behind him for his gun and pointed it at the girls. "In fact, the two of you are still our prey. Perhaps I've forgotten some of my own lessons. Don't converse with your dinner."

"You're going to sacrifice your own son?" Kathy asked. "You truly don't value life at all, do you?"

"Honey, you should be thankful I didn't let my son do to you what he's done to all the other female game we've gone after." He cocked the gun. "And Kurt, I'm sorry. You were a good son. For a while."

Several tense seconds passed as Samantha, Donovan, and Kathy all prepared for the execution that was about to happen.

"Wait!" Kurt nearly shrieked. "Wait. I know where the little girl's mother is."

"What little girl?" Jim asked.

"The one who we never found last week," Kurt said. "The one you thought would die from starvation. She's alive. I just saw her. And I know where her mother is. She's alive too."

CHAPTER 28

- 1987 -

Donovan grinned from ear to ear as he chased his latest prey through the woods. He felt invigorated. Alive.

"She's coming up to your section, Kurt," he spoke into the walkie talkie.

"Copy that."

Changing course, Donovan came up to the tree stand they had hidden and climbed up the ladder quickly. The woman was fast approaching and if she saw him, the plan would need to be altered on the fly.

Plans on the fly never went well.

Donovan made it to the top without being spotted. He looked out beneath him. Being the middle of October, some trees had shed all of their leaves while others still boasted vibrant, beautiful warm colors that contrasted the nip in the air.

The temporary reprieve was enough for Donovan. He had been working all week with his uncle and his cousins, building cabins on Uncle Jim's property for a little side business. Who wouldn't want to enjoy the beautiful Allegheny Mountains, just like this? The leaves, the beautiful views on the trails that snaked through the property, and the stream that ran through it all. It was truly paradise, in Donovan's opinion.

The walkie crackled and Pete's voice came on. "She's in position."

Donovan smiled. Their plan was taking shape.

He peered down and saw her.

Their prey approached quickly, throwing her head back to eye her pursuers coming up behind her. Facing forward again, she hadn't regained her bearings enough to notice the bear trap laying beneath the fallen leaves. Waiting for her.

The trap snapped shut around her leg and the woman let out a piercing shriek into the fall sky.

"Got her," Donovan said into the walkie. He slowly began to climb down the ladder. He assumed she had seen him because she let out another shriek and he heard the clang of metal as she tried to escape the trap.

As if she could.

By the time he laid eyes on her, he saw that her leg had been broken. Nearly snapped in two. But based on the terror in her eyes, adrenaline was preventing her from feeling the full extent of the pain.

That would change.

Blood lay around her and coated her skin. She lay on her back and frantically tried to back away, but the tug of the trap held her in place.

Pete and Kurt arrived from different positions.

"Nice!" Kurt cheered.

"Good idea with the bear trap, Don," Pete said.

"I wasn't sure if it would snap her leg right off," he said. "Either way, we got her. She's not going anywhere." He knelt down beside her and started poking at her injured leg, but she recoiled in pain.

"Don't touch that!" Uncle Jim's voice boomed behind Donovan. "The damn thing could be carrying diseases. You don't want the bitch to get you sick, do you?"

Donovan wiped her blood from his finger onto some dry leaves and rose back up to standing. "No, I guess not."

"Please!" the woman said through tears. "Let me go! I'll find a way out of the woods, and I promise, I won't tell a soul!"

Uncle Jim shook his head. "See, we can't do that. We're not stupid. Say you do manage to get out here without getting a massive infection in your leg—or worse, getting killed by bears or coyotes. Let's pretend for a minute that you *do* manage to get out of here. No matter who finds you, they're going to take you to a hospital, and you know what's going to happen then?"

She shook her head, her eyes locked on his.

"They start asking *questions* about how you got hurt and who did this to you. And let's say that you actually *will* hold up your promise and keep this a secret, there's nothing you can do to stop a police investigation into your assault. They're going to track your whereabouts and figure out you were on my property and then they're going to come knocking on *my* door asking me *questions*." He shook his head. "Nope. Can't have that. You wanna know why?"

The woman cowered as Jim leaned in close to her.

"Because we're having too much fun." He backed away and roared with laughter. "No. You're going to die." He pulled his pistol from its holster and pointed it at her. "The question is, are we going to shoot you for a quick death, or are we going to beat you just like we do any other critter that gets caught in one of our traps?"

The girl studied him, shaking.

Kurt rubbed his hands together. "Can I play with her first?"

"Get a grip, Kurt," Pete snapped. "And keep it in your pants."

"Now, now," Jim said. "Your brother has a right to his fun. And you'll have yours too. When your brother is done with her, you can go at her with your knife. But don't kill her—I think Donovan is the one who should do the honors there. The bear trap *was* his idea."

The woman whimpered when all the men seemed to smile

at the idea of the slow and excruciating horrors she was about to endure.

"But I would like you to take the shot from up there." Jim pointed up to the tree stand in the branches. "You still need to work on your precision skills with the rifle."

Donovan nodded. "Yes, sir. I've been practicing."

"Well good!" Jim patted his nephew on the shoulder. "And I'm excited to see how you've improved. But first, let your cousins have fun with her. Don't you think they've earned it for helping nab this one?"

Donovan nodded.

The woman was sobbing now. Her face was a wet, ugly mess. "Please!" Her voice was strained with terror and sadness. "Don't do this! I want to live! My parents will come looking for me! You've already killed my boyfriend. They won't ignore—"

Jim hit her in the face the butt of his pistol. "Shut your mouth! The way your parents will see it, your little boyfriend came out here to kill himself. Single gunshot to the head. Gunpowder residue on his hand and everything. As for you." He leaned in close to her again. "There won't be a trace of you to find."

"No!" she roared in his face.

Jim stood, unfazed by her outburst. He snapped his fingers in her direction, but looked at the boys. "Get to work. This one needs to be put down sooner than later."

Kurt approached with a big smile on his face. The same look

he used to get every Christmas morning.

“Come on.” Jim led Pete and Donovan a few feet away, their back turned on the woman and Kurt. “Let’s give them some privacy.”

Kurt unzipped his pants as he hovered over the woman. “We’re going to have fun, sweetheart. Just hold still.”

CHAPTER 29

"You think I care about the vermin that escaped?" Jim asked. "If you have her held captive and we can't find her, she'll die of starvation anyway." His hand tightened on the gun.

"Wait!" Samantha called. "Where is she?"

"Let's say we make a deal?" Kurt suggested. "Her whereabouts for my freedom."

That seemed to get Jim's attention, and he lowered his gun.

"Tell us where she is," Kathy said.

"You're in no position to make demands, lady!" Donovan said.

"I have your cousin tied up and about to be executed by your father," Kathy said. "I think I'm in a perfect position." She grabbed Kurt by the collar. "Tell us!"

You sound too desperate, Samantha warned.

Kathy glared at her sister. *Would you rather explain to Crystal how we weren't able to save her mother?*

Samantha was telepathically quiet.

"I'll tell you this much," Kurt said. "Ever since I caught her, she's been a special toy of mine. Been pretty good too, for a sad prisoner who is going to die."

Kathy clenched her jaw. Her mind ran wild with the terrors this woman, who she had never met, must have experienced.

Then, an idea struck her.

Scan his mind, she tried to think the words as "loud" as she could so her sister would pick up on it.

What? Samantha asked.

Good, she had "heard" her. *Scan his mind and see if you can pull the information he's withholding from us. That way, we can let Jim kill him and go save Crystal's mother.*

I'll try, Samantha thought back.

Before she could start, though, Rick's screams radiated out from the barn again. A moment later, he ran out into the driveway, shirtless and bloody with Pete hot on his tail.

"Rick!" Kathy called to him. "Get to the woods!"

Before he had a chance to get his bearings with the standoff in the driveway, Donovan sprung into action and tackled him down to the gravel.

Instinct took over and Kathy broke away from her sister's

side to run to Rick's aid. Swinging her leg around, she kicked Donovan hard in the side. He swatted at her and tried to fight her off from his position on the ground while she stood over him.

Both of them were oblivious to Jim having turned to point his gun at them. Already cocked and loaded, all he needed to do was squeeze the trigger.

"Drop it!" Samantha warned. She had raised the gun in her own hand so it was pointing at Jim now.

Kurt shot to his feet and ran to Pete. "Untie me!"

Pete ignored his brother and ran to where Rick was slowly picking himself off the ground. The bloody knife he had pulled from his belt loop glimmered as he moved.

Kathy pushed Donovan away long enough to grab Rick's hand and help hurl him up to his feet. Pete's knife narrowly missed striking Rick's skin again in a last-ditch effort to stop them.

"Are you okay?" Kathy asked him as she pulled him further away from the growing chaos of the crowd. Her eyes scanned over his body. There were lots of cuts and scraps. A few deeper gouges. All of it bleeding out. But, luckily, for the most part, they were surface wounds. Likely because Pete wanted information out of him about Samantha and Kathy's whereabouts. He hadn't intended to kill him. Not yet, at least.

Once she had confirmed that Rick was okay, Kathy turned back to the rest of the crowd. She raised her hands to freeze, but the door of the main house swung open and out walked Sue.

Without missing a beat, Sue slammed the frying pan she held in her hand down hard on Samantha's head, who stood just at the bottom of the porch steps.

Kathy's heart raced fast as she watched her sister drop to the gravel. With the force that Sue had hit her, Kathy worried that her sister was seriously hurt. But first she needed to save her.

"That's enough rough housing!" Sue called out in a tone that meant she would not entertain anyone questioning her.

Her presence made Kathy hesitate. Did Sue know exactly what the boys were doing? What kind of woman would allow these vicious acts to continue if she had known about it? What kind of woman would allow children to run in fear? Mothers to be separated from their children?

"But Mom," Pete started. "These are the ones we've been—"

She swung the frying pan in front of her. "I don't want to hear it! Move it to the woods where I can't hear you or I'll bop you all on the head just like I did this one."

"Sam." Kathy spoke under her breath and moved with tunnel vision, focused only on her sister's limp body. She was pulled out of her trance when something—or someone—tugged on her arm.

"Kathy, don't."

She looked back. It was Rick. He held her arm and was trying to lead her back to the woods.

"But…I have to get my—I can't just leave her!" Kathy

struggled against him and tried to get to Samantha.

"You won't be able to save her if we're *dead*," Rick said. "You saved me. Now let me save you."

Kathy followed his eyes and saw the Fishers closing in on them with hunger in their eyes.

"Now's our chance," Rick hissed.

"Go on!" Sue called out to her family. "Get the hell out of here! I've been hearing that damn screaming for the last hour!" She glanced down at Samantha's crumpled form as if it were rotting garbage. "And clean this one up and get her out of here! The last thing we need around here is more junk."

The Fisher men turned to obey Sue's orders and turned their backs to Kathy and Rick.

"Let's go." Rick's voice was right near Kathy's ear, but as she stood by and watched those monsters pick up her sister's helpless body and carry her into the house, it was as if Rick was standing a thousand miles away.

With more tugging and prodding, Rick finally got Kathy to move and ushered her back into the woods. Once they were under the cover of the trees, they took off at a run to get away from the Fisher house as fast as possible.

CHAPTER 30

They ran until Kathy noticed that they were getting too far away from the supply barn. Samantha might have been captured, but Kathy was not about to let Crystal sit scared any longer.

"Wait!" Kathy pointed. "We have to go this way."

"What? No. We have to keep going. We have to regroup and come up with a plan first."

Kathy shook her head. "Crystal is hiding out in the barn we found all the supplies in. She's scared, Rick, and we need to protect her."

He put his hands on his hips as he weighed both options. Sweat glistened down his bare chest from running—and fear—and mixed with the blood that was dripping from his wounds.

Kathy seemed to just notice it. "You're still bleeding!"

Rick glanced down at himself, as if he just noticed it for the first time himself. "I guess I am. Running made my blood pump faster."

"We have to get you cleaned up." She grabbed his arm and directed him toward the supply barn. "We can find some supplies to help with those wounds—and get you a shirt."

"That's...probably a good idea," he admitted. "Are you saying you don't want to see me without a shirt?"

Kathy smirked at him. "No comment. Can we focus on getting my sister back?"

He nodded as they continued walking at a slower pace now. "Yeah. Sorry about that."

"Why are *you* sorry? You didn't knock her on the head with a frying pan."

"No, but I did run in there like a wild man, despite your justified objections."

"Is that your way of saying I was right?"

He glanced down at her. "Not if that's your way of saying 'I told you so.'"

"Fair enough. But I'd like to get my sister back. In one piece, preferably." When she heard her words out loud, she cringed. "Sorry. I didn't mean to—"

"I know. It's fine." He kept his eyes diverted on the ground as they walked. "But if there's one thing we've both learned, it's that running in without a solid plan is stupid and going to get us killed, just like they want. We need a plan."

"I have a feeling you have one formulating already."

He nodded. "I didn't finish putting the explosives around the barn like I wanted to, but I did finish putting them around the house. And since they caught me running to the barn and *not* by the house, I bet they don't even realize that their house is a ticking bomb."

"The bomb is on a timer?"

"No. It was a figure of speech. My point is, the explosives are planted around their house. Now all we need is to make sure they're in there when we light the match."

Kathy's eyes widened as she looked up at him. "You are *not* going to set off those explosives with Samantha inside!"

He sighed. "I'm going to try not to, but if the opportunity arises, I have to—"

"*No*, Rick." She stopped in her tracks and turned to him. "Don't forget that I can stop you if I need to."

"If you mess this up, then we'll be on the run forever. Even *if* you manage to get your sister out of there and you *don't* kill them, we'll always be looking over our shoulders. You go back to the city and the Fishers will follow you. In fact, that might even *increase* the thrill of the hunt for them." Rick shook his head. "I don't like it, but this is the only way."

Kathy crossed her arms and cast her eyes aside, landing on the bleeding slits in Rick's body. Beneath the blood, sweat, and dirt, she could see that he had a very nice form. Not that sex was at the top of her mind at the moment.

She let out a deep breath. "We have to get you cleaned up. Come on, the barn isn't much further."

They were quiet as they walked the few minutes back to the barn. Once Kathy had scoped out the outside—which took some convincing of Rick, who thought he was better equipped as a man before she reminded him that she was a witch who could stop time—she quietly opened the sliding barn doors for her and Rick to step through.

Rick closed the doors behind them once they were inside.

"Better to show no trace that we were here," he said. "In case they decide to show up. There's a chance we could slip out the back undetected. Or you could freeze them so we can escape."

Kathy nodded. "You find some clean clothes and a first aid kit. I'm going to go up and get Crystal, then I'll be down to help you with those cuts."

"I can get it."

She stopped and grabbed his hands to get his attention. "Let me help. We need to trust each other, right?"

Their eyes met, then he conceded to her. "Okay. I'll find some clothes first. I should be able to find my bag in the dark."

The barn only had one window up near the eave of the roof. It let in a lot of light, but there were still many dim corners in the old barn with the sliding doors closed.

Kathy climbed up the ladder. "Crystal? Are you still up here?"

Silence.

"Crystal!" Her voice was louder. Shakier as fear crept into her tone. "It's me. Kathy. Come on out. It's safe."

"What's the password?" The small voice traveled from a corner where the eave of the roof met the floor of the loft. In front of her was a stack of hay that Kathy guessed had been pushed there by Crystal herself.

Smart girl.

"The password is cucumber." Kathy could feel the relief wash over her. Crystal was safe. Leaving her was something both Samantha and Kathy hated to do. At least one of them had come back to her.

"Where's Samantha?" Crystal crawled out from behind the hay.

"Let's go downstairs so we can talk," Kathy suggested.

"She's dead, isn't she?" Crystal's bottom lip pouted out and her shoulders began to shake.

"No, she's not, honey." Kathy reached for the girl and pulled her into her lap and coddled her like a baby.

"Then where is she?" Crystal's tear-streaked face pierced through any wall of deception that Kathy was about to use.

"Uh…well…" Kathy glanced down to the main floor of the barn, where Rick was pulling on a flannel shirt.

He shrugged his shoulders, as if to say, *What do you want me to do?*

Turning back to the girl, Kathy decided on the truth.

"Well…the Fishers have her."

"What!"

"But!" Kathy gripped the girl's shoulders to steady her. "We're going to get her back. We just need to work out a plan."

A warning look came her way from Rick down below.

Crystal cried harder. "Samantha is going to end up just like my mom and dad!"

"No, honey! No. We're not going to let anything happen to her. We're going to get her back. I promise."

"You said that they are crazy. They'll do anything."

Kathy moved the hair out of Crystal's face and wiped away a tear. "We're *going* to get Samantha back. That's a promise. And, we're going to find your mom."

"You are?"

She nodded. "Yes. We know someone who knows what happened to her."

Crystal smiled at that. She wrapped her arms around Kathy and hugged her tightly. "I can't wait!"

Over Crystal's shoulder, Kathy exchanged worried looks with Rick. Either they were going to find out what happened to Crystal's mother, or they were going to die.

CHAPTER 31

"Ah, that stings!" Rick winced as Kathy used a liberal amount of rubbing alcohol on his wounds.

She took quiet satisfaction in the fact that he was in pain.

Good, she thought. *Let him be.*

Pouring a little more on a piece of the T-shirt Rick had ripped up for a clean rag, she pressed it against another one of his scrapes and rubbed harder than necessary.

Again, he winced. "You're enjoying this, aren't you?"

"Hmm?" She shrugged. "Don't you deserve it?"

His eyebrows raised. "Are you kidding me?"

She kept her eyes locked on her work. "You're the one who got us into this mess in the first place."

He pulled away in order to get her attention. "Seriously? You're blaming *me* for this?"

"Not *all* of it. Just the current situation. If it hadn't been for you running in all bull-headed, then we wouldn't have had to save you, and Samantha wouldn't be tied up at their house."
Rick took a deep breath and forced himself to lower his voice. "You know why I rushed in like that. It obviously wasn't my smartest choice, but don't sit there and lie to me that you wouldn't have done the same thing if it was someone *you* cared about."

Kathy tossed the rag down on the dirty floor of the barn and crossed her arms. "Like my *sister*? And yet, here I am, cleaning *you* up because I know we need a solid plan before we go in to save her. And, like it or not, I know that the only chance I'll have of getting her out alive is by using your help."

Rick licked his lips and nodded again. "I know. And I'm sorry."

The two for them studied each other for a long moment. Kathy tried not to let her eyes wander to his half-naked body. She wanted to have a reason to touch him again, but knew it was better to keep her distance. They had more pressing things at the moment, like saving Samantha.

He leaned in closer, and Kathy felt an almost gravitational pull toward him as well.

In a near-silent voice, he asked, "What are we going to do?"

Kathy looked confused until she saw Rick nod in Crystal's

direction. The little girl was walking up and down the rows of items the Fishers had stolen from their previous victims. Kathy had told her to look for food, more first-aid kits, clothes that would fit, anything that might be able to help them. At the moment, she was oblivious that Rick and Kathy were talking in such quiet tones.

"Do you think Kurt really knows where her mom is?" he finished. "If she even *is* alive."

Kathy sighed and watched Crystal for a little bit. Then she turned back to Rick. "I don't know, but we need to make every effort to find her. She deserves a happy ending to all of this."

"I still don't understand why you can't just snap your fingers and get Samantha back."

"I told you. It doesn't work like that. My power is only to stop time. And even then, only for a short while, and only a few people *in* time." She shook her head. "I'm not powerful enough to control *all* of time."

"So you can't read the Fishers' minds to tell if they're even lying?" he asked.

"Actually, that's Samantha's power." Kathy reached for a roll of gauze and began to wrap it around Rick's body, trying to cover the worst of his scraps.

"And what did she find?" Rick asked. His arms were raised above him while Kathy worked the gauze around his torso. Both of them pretended not to notice the intimacy of the situation.

"I don't know. If she even tried to read their minds, she was taken before she could tell me."

Rick nodded. "Even more reason to get her back."

They were standing very close now. Kathy could feel the heat of his body radiating off of him. Then again, her own body temperature had raised higher than normal. She needed to get out into the cool air again.

Suddenly, Rick stiffened. Kathy's eyes scanned his body, worried that she had bumped something to cause him pain. But when she looked him in the eyes, she saw his face was more serious. Thoughtful.

"What is it?" she asked.

"I just remembered something. When I was looking for my own shelter, I found a dugout shelter that looked to be one of those cold storage cellars from back in the day. That's how I got the idea to dig out my own shelter. I didn't want to stay in one that was there because I didn't know if the Fishers already knew about it."

"Okay, so…" Kathy wanted him to get to the point.

"So I wonder if that's where Kurt is keeping Crystal's mother." His voice fell to a low whisper again.

Kathy perked up. "Do you think you can find it again?"

"I should be able to," he said. "It was down near the creek. Almost by Cabin 8. If we go now, we should be able to get there before he does—"

"Wait." She grabbed his arm to keep him from getting up. "Should we rescue her first or Samantha first?"

Rick considered. "I think we need to rescue her first. We *know* Samantha is in the Fisher house with the whole family. Like I said, if we hurry, we might be able to get to the dugout cellar and rescue—" He cast his eyes to the corner where Crystal had stopped to dig through a suitcase, then leaned in and lowered his voice. "Crystal's mother before Kurt comes back for her. And you know he'll want to get rid of her when he does."

Kathy nodded. Her heart ached with the idea of leaving Samantha in that house for even longer. But Kathy had to agree that it was the right path forward. "Okay. What do we need?"

CHAPTER 32

Samantha's head was groggy when she came to. The first thing she felt—besides the throbbing in her head—was that her hands and feet were tied to the chair she was sitting in. Upon further consideration, she felt something stuck to the side of her face. Dried blood, she had to guess. Which would also explain the throbbing headache.

Slowly, she opened her eyes and saw all the Fishers standing around the kitchen. Samantha recognized the room she was in as the dining room. The same room she and Kathy had signed the rental agreement papers when they had first arrived.

Despite her efforts, it was hard for her to keep her eyes open. She fought against the urge to close them.

Focus, she told herself.

With effort, she was able to allow her eyes to adjust enough that it was no longer painful to look into the kitchen, although it was still a little difficult to follow the conversation.

She tried to feel around their minds telepathically, but again, their thoughts blurred together and only contributed to the ache in her skull.

"So then what are we going to do?" a voice asked in the next room.

It sounded familiar. The name was on the tip of Samantha's tongue, at the forefront of her mind, but she just couldn't—

Donovan! That's who it was.

"Yeah," another voice asked. Pete. "We've never brought one into the house after we've started hunting."

"Doesn't that go against one of your rules?" Kurt asked.

"Boys," Sue scolded. "Leave your father alone. He's under a lot of stress."

"But Mom!" Pete whined. "You can't tell me you want that *rodent* in our house anymore than I do!"

Samantha glanced around the well-loved and worn room with packaging boxes, animal pelts, muddy shoes, and mounts on the wall. This was certainly not a palace. And she was definitely not a rodent.

"Would you all *shut up*!" Jim barked.

The room fell silent. The tension in the room was thick. Even Samantha felt nervous to even move, afraid that his anger would suddenly turn on her if he knew she was awake.

"We need to get the loose ones first," he finally said. "The ones who've run out into the woods. And we can't let any of them escape and presume they'll die. Obviously that hasn't worked for us with these ones."

"All of them?" Kurt asked in a quiet voice.

"Even the little girl?" Pete added.

Shoot, Samantha thought to herself. *How do they know about Crystal? Unless they're counting bodies...*

"Every single one of them," Jim said.

"Wouldn't it be easier to kill this one and hang her outside until they come running, crying, and trying to get revenge?" Donovan asked. "She would be the perfect bait."

"Donovan," Sue said with a gasp. "That's *sick*. Do you think I want that unsightly thing hanging outside my house? And to have that blood mess in the driveway. It would take *months* to clear it up!"

"Yeah, but then they would come to us," Donovan pleaded. "And we wouldn't have to—"

Something hard slammed down with a sudden jolt that made even Samantha jump with fear. Judging by the sound, she presumed it was the frying pan she had been hit with. This time, colliding with the countertop.

"I said we're going after the loose ones first!" Jim barked in a tone that was not meant to be questioned. "Now get the hell out of here and load up the damn truck!"

"Yes, sir," Pete said as he started for the door.

Samantha saw him step into the dining room and he laid eyes on her. He knew she was awake now.

"Uh…we can go hunting, but would it be okay if I took care of something quick first?" Kurt asked in the kitchen, oblivious to Pete's finding. "Half hour, tops. And then I'll be ready to go."

Jim let out a heavy sigh. "It'll take the boys that long to load up the truck anyway. I suppose you can go. But not a minute longer."

How quickly they had slipped back into the father-son role when a little more than an hour ago Jim was willing to kill his own son, Samantha thought.

Kurt brushed by his brother on the way out the door.

"Why'd you let him go?" Pete asked.

"Yeah, and why do we need to load up the truck?" Donovan added.

"Because that's what I said," Jim told them. "Kurt has a woman stashed somewhere. We all have our souvenirs from our hunts, right? Kurt's just happen to have an expiration date. The least we can do is let him have some time with his before we make him kill it."

It, Samantha thought. *Crystal's mother has been reduced to an 'it.' No wonder they feel no remorse for killing people.*

"Get out of here and load up the truck!" Jim ordered.

Pete and Donovan ran out of the house without anymore objections.

"Go easy on them," Sue said to her husband when the boys

were gone. "They adore you. They're only trying to make you happy."

"And I'm just trying to keep them safe," he said. "To keep us all safe."

Samantha heard footsteps and quickly dropped her head and closed her eyes, pretending to still be knocked out.

Something rough and hard smacked her cheek, sending shockwaves throughout her throbbing head.

"Wake up, bitch." Jim leaned over in front of her. He smiled a yellow, toothy smile, and said, "We're going to have some fun once we round up the rest of you."

CHAPTER 33

- 1987 -

Jim used a shovel to scoop up the skin that had been removed. He deposited it into a plastic trash bin. Later, he and the boys would have to take it out back and dump it for the animals to pick at. It would draw them in so that the boys would have successful animal hunts in between human hunts.

Pete worked his knife as he carved the rest of the meat off the girl. She hung on a hook in the barn across the driveway from their house.

This was a part of the process that always made Jim nervous, although he never shared that fear with his family. If anyone were to show up at their property and peer inside the barn, there would be a lot of explaining to do. Luckily, the Fishers didn't get very many visitors. Not yet, anyway.

The sound of tires on gravel drew Jim's attention outside. His heart beat faster when he saw a Warren County Sheriff car pull up and park just beside Jim's truck. The same truck he and the boys had used to bring the girl back up to the barn.

"Stay here," Jim told the boys. "And start cleaning up. Just in case."

Donovan and Kurt peered through the sliding door, but Jim closed it as he exited. He noticed that his hands were stained red from the girl's blood.

"Evening, Officer," Jim said with a smile. "Is there something I can help you with?"

The sheriff deputy noticed Jim's hands.

"Oh," he said with a smirk. "You'll have to excuse this. The boys and I just went hunting. We've been prepping the meat for meals." Best to stay as honest as possible.

The deputy seemed to relax. "Your freezer should be full with all the animals running around out here."

"Sure is," Jim said. "So what brings you out to my neck of the woods?" He walked over to the porch on the house and took a seat on the steps. It was a move meant to indicate casualness, but in reality Jim just wanted the deputy to face *away* from the barn where the boys were dismembering a woman.

"Well, we're following up on some calls from a missing couple," the deputy said. "A boy and a girl. Their families said they were out here camping over the weekend. Supposed to return Sunday afternoon. Haven't been seen since."

"How old?"

"Mid-twenties, judging from the pictures they shared." The deputy pulled a photo from his pocket and held it up to Jim. "They look familiar?"

Jim forced himself not to react. The picture was of the couple they had killed—first the boyfriend, who they shot at point-blank range to scare the girl to run, then the girlfriend, who was currently being torn apart only twenty feet away.

"No, haven't seen them," Jim lied. "Were they camping around here? What kind of camping and wilderness experience did they have? You have to be careful of bears out here."

The deputy put the picture back in his pocket. "No idea. In fact, we think they may have just gone somewhere else for the weekend instead. What young couple goes camping in this weather? If you ask me, this is a case of overprotected parents who've had the wool pulled over their eyes."

The cool air seemed to send a chill down Jim's back. "Right. Well, if I see them, I'll let you know."

"I appreciate that," the deputy said, "but if it's all the same, I'd like to see the records of your cabin rentals, just to be sure. I'm sure my supervisor will double-check that I've looked into this to the fullest extent possible."

Jim nodded. "Sure. Sue takes care of all of that. She's inside." He stood and led the deputy into the house. "You know, we only have three cabins built so far. The boys and I envision ten total, dotted along the property. Enough to bring in an income, but not too many so that our quiet little oasis becomes a tourist destination."

"I get that. It's so beautiful out here, I'm sure you'll have no problem doing business."

"Sue!" Jim called inside. "There's a sheriff deputy who would like to speak to us!"

His wife poked her head into the room from around the corner. The sound of the hood vent above the stove roared behind her. "I'm in the kitchen, fixing dinner."

Jim nodded in her direction and led the deputy to the kitchen. "This gentleman has questions about a couple he thinks stayed here. He's afraid something might've happened to them. I said that you handle all of that."

The deputy pulled the picture out again and set it on the counter in front of Sue. She looked at it, then looked at Jim, then back at the picture, then at the deputy. "What happened to them?"

"We're not sure," the deputy said. "All we know is that they never returned home when they said they did. Have you seen them?"

Sue swallowed, then nodded. "They just checked out on Sunday."

The deputy looked at Jim, catching him in the lie.

"They did?" Jim asked. "I never saw them. Are you sure?"

Sue nodded. "Definitely. They arrived late, after dinner. You had fallen asleep in front of the TV already. And then they checked out while you and the boys were hunting. I remember telling them that it was...*improper* for a boy and a girl to be staying in the same cabin if they weren't married. They basically told me to butt out. It was such an unpleasant experience that I never mentioned it. I try not to dwell on bad people."

The deputy nodded. "Do you have a record of their stay? Or an approximate time that they checked out?"

"I have the paperwork." She handed Jim the spoon and waved to the pot. "Stir that so it doesn't burn."

Jim dutifully went to the pot and began stirring the stew. He touched only the end of the spoon, careful not to get blood on anything that would touch their food.

"That smells good. Is that venison?" the deputy asked.

Jim simply nodded. "It's from our latest hunt." His eyes traveled to the picture on the counter. The young man smiling in the picture was being cooked up on the stove right in front of the sheriff.

Sue came back a moment later with a few papers in her hands. "Here they are. They signed out on Sunday just after eleven in the morning." She handed them to the deputy, who looked them over.

"Mind if I hold on to these?"

Sue made a face. "If you don't mind, I'd like to hold on to them. They're our only copy and we like to keep them for tax records."

The deputy pulled out a notepad from his chest pocket. “Okay. Let me just jot down the dates and times. I know where to find you if I need to get ahold of these again.” He scribbled on the notepad, then handed the paperwork back to Sue. “Thank you.”

“I hope they’re okay,” Sue added. “Sinners or not, everyone is worthy of forgiveness.”

“I’m going to do my best to find out what happened to them,” the deputy said. “Thank you both for your time. You should keep an eye out for them, though. With the amount of land you guys own, it’s possible that they got lost somewhere on your property.”

Jim shook his head. “I don’t think so. The boys and I wander the full property often. But we’ll be sure to keep an eye out and call you if we see anything. Do you have a card?”

The deputy pulled one out of his pocket and set it on the counter. “I appreciate you looking. I’ll be in touch if I need anything else. And, please, call me if you see something.”

Jim picked up the card. “Will do.”

The Fishers led him to the door and stood on the porch as he walked back to his car. Husband and wife stood next to each other in silence as they watched the sheriff deputy pull out of the driveway.

When he was gone, Jim said, “We need to be more careful. Maybe we shouldn’t have records of the guests we hunt. It only shows that they were here and implicates us.”

“Do you think he’ll be back?”

“I don’t think so. But we’ll have to be more careful in the future.”

CHAPTER 34

"Are you sure you know where we're going?" Kathy lingered several feet behind Rick so she could keep pace with Crystal, who was tired of walking. The little girl had only complained a few times, and Kathy admired her strength.

"Yes. I told you, it's around here somewhere." Rick peered at the base of each tree.

"Well, we've been walking for an hour and I feel like we're going in circles," Kathy said.

Crystal pointed. "I think we've passed that same rock three times."

"Would you—" Rick started to snap, but when he turned and saw Crystal, he stopped himself.

Kathy put her arm around the girl. "It's okay. We're all just tired and frustrated."

Rick continued searching, stepping carefully through the fallen leaves.

"Why aren't we going back to help Samantha?" Crystal asked once they began following again. "I wish she was here."

"Me too," Kathy said. "Trust me. We'll save her. I promise."

It was like a reflex. Kathy couldn't stop promising things to Crystal in an effort to comfort her, even though she had no idea whether they actually *would* save her. But Kathy was certainly going to die trying.

The faint sound of a woman's voice echoed through the woods. Kathy almost couldn't hear it over the crunch of leaves beneath their feet and the wind blowing through the trees. But in the few moments of silence, she heard it.

"Did you hear that?" Kathy asked Rick.

"Shh." He put a finger to his lips. Everyone stopped in their tracks, listening intently.

Then they heard it again. Clearer this time.

Screams.

Crystal latched herself onto Kathy and whimpered in fear.

Kathy rubbed her back and leaned over to squeeze her. "Shh. It's okay." She glanced up at Rick, who looked just as confused as Kathy felt.

The screams sounded again and Rick sprung into action. He ran in the direction they came from. Kathy took a step forward, but was held back by Crystal's arms clinging to her.

There he goes, running off without a plan again, Kathy thought.

"Come on, sweetie, we have to help Rick."

"No!" Crystal dug her feet into the ground and pulled back as Kathy tried to lead her to the sound of the scream.

"I'll protect you. I won't let anything bad happen to you. I haven't let you down yet, have I?" There she was again, making promises she wasn't sure she could keep.

Either way, it let the girl's guard down and she slowly eased her resistance and followed alongside Kathy, hand locked in hers.

They caught up to Rick just as he came upon the cellar they'd been looking for. No wonders they hadn't spotted it. The door was buried at the base of a tree, covered in moss and hidden under fallen leaves.

Rick pulled it open without hesitation and the sound of the scream erupted even louder.

"Wait, we don't know—" Kathy's warnings were ignored. He hurried down, gun raised and ready to shoot. "Rick, damn it, don't be an idiot!"

When Kathy tried to follow, she was again held back by Crystal clinging to her in fear.

"Wait here," she told the girl in a harsher tone than she

intended. But she took advantage of Crystal's shock in her tone and the effect it had on the hold the girl had on her, and darted down the stairs after Rick.

Just as Rick had described it before, it was an old cooling shelter. There were several candles burning in the corner to provide light, but the space was cold and damp.

In the faint light, it took Kathy's eyes a while to adjust, but when they did she saw Kurt on top of a woman in the corner. She screamed and tried to fight him off, but her efforts were meek. It was as if she lacked the strength necessary for her basic survival instincts to kick in. Rick hesitated a few feet away. Probably trying to get his bearings so that he knew what he was doing when he acted.

Decision made, Rick ran up and kicked Kurt hard in the side.

"Get off her, you pervert!" he shouted.

Kurt grunted as he fell, but quickly recovered and got to his feet. He zipped up his pants, then reached for his gun from his back pocket.

With the men occupied, Kathy took the opportunity to run up to the woman and help her up. When their hands touched, Kathy could tell just how thin her arm was. Upon closer inspection, she saw the woman had been tied to the wall. Her clothes were filthy and worn. She had been here for a while.

"Rick, a little help here," Kathy called to him as he and Kurt squared off.

"Don't you touch her, you bitch!" Kurt snapped.

Kathy ignored him.

"What do you need?" Rick kept his eyes locked on his opponent.

"Something sharp. It's only rope."

Rick continued to study Kurt while he pulled a large knife out of his pocket and slid it across the floor in Kathy's direction. She snapped it up quickly and got to work.

The rope was thick, but it was old and damp too. Worn. Kathy found a notch and began sawing frantically at it. When she was about halfway, there was a loud bang and then her ears seemed to implode, followed by a dull ringing sound in her head.

Gunshot.

Her eyes snapped up to check that Rick was okay. He was. And so was Kurt. Judging by their positions, Kurt had made the shot, but Rick had dived out of the way.

"You okay?" Kathy called.

"Just peachy," he said as he picked himself up. "You about done?"

"Getting there."

Rick lunged at Kurt, tackling him to the ground. Metal struck the cold brick floor and Kathy heard the distinct sound of the gun sliding away from one of them. She was too focused on her work with the rope to notice who had lost their weapon, but she hoped Rick had the upper hand.

"Thank you." The woman's voice was small, almost inaudible. Her eyes fluttered half-open as she faded in and out of consciousness.

"Of course." Kathy smiled at her as she worked. "What's your name?"

"Lynn."

"Do you..." Kathy grunted as she sawed through more fibers on the rope. "Do you have a daughter? About eight or nine?"

Lynn lit up at that. "Yes! Yes, I do! Her name is Crystal."

Kathy smiled. "We've got her. She's safe." As soon as the words left her mouth, she hoped they were true. She hoped that Crystal was waiting safely outside. But with the girl out of sight, she couldn't be sure.

"Oh, thank you!" Lynn began to cry.

The rope finally severed.

"Got it!" Kathy called.

Rick had gotten on top of Kurt and was punching him in the face. At the sound of Kathy's voice, he paused, for only a moment, to glance in her direction, and that's when Kurt took advantage of the weakness and brought both hands together into a double fist and drove them straight into Rick's gut.

He fell to the cold floor as Kurt got to his feet and retrieved his gun. He pointed it at Rick, then at Kathy and Lynn, then back at Rick, alternating his position every few seconds to keep them all at bay.

"Don't move!" Kurt demanded. "Or I'll shoot you all! Now, that old bitch has been getting kind of boring. But you—" He pointed his gun at Kathy. "—you look healthy. You look *fun*. I'll trade her for you!"

There was a shadow that appeared in the doorway. Kathy held her breath. Was that the rest of the Fishers, coming down to kill what was left of their victims?

"Mommy!"

The sound of Crystal's voice made Kathy's blood turn cold. She would've almost rather had seen one of the Fishers.

Oblivious to the dangerous situation, the little girl ran down the stairs and toward her mother, but Kurt caught the hem of her shirt and pulled her toward him.

"No!" the girl squealed.

"Don't touch her!" Lynn cried out in a ragged breath.

"Let her go!" Rick demanded. He pointed his gun at Kurt. He must've picked it up in the momentary chaos of Crystal's entry.

Kurt pressed the gun to the back of Crystal's head.

Lynn sank to her knees. "Please! Please, just let her go! She's just a child! She doesn't deserve this! She doesn't deserve any of this! Take me! I'll go with you willingly! I'll do anything! Just don't hurt my baby girl."

"I don't want you back." Kurt turned his face down, disgusted by the idea. "Didn't you hear? I need fresh meat."

"She's only eight years old," Kathy said.

"If you say another word, the girl dies."

Crystal whimpered in his grip.

Kathy looked over at Rick for assistance. He glanced in her direction as well. Kathy nodded toward Kurt and Crystal. Rick gave one quick nod in acknowledgement.

He fired his gun.

Lynn screamed.

Kurt's eyes widened in surprise.

Kathy froze the room.

For a moment, she sat in the silence and paused tension. She took a deep breath, then sprang into action.

The first thing she did was pull Crystal from Kurt's grasp, which unfroze the girl.

"What happened?" she asked. "What's going on? What happened to my mom?"

"Crystal, listen to me." Kathy put her hands on the girl's shoulders. "Take your mom by the hand. She'll wake up when you touch her. Take her upstairs and *stay up there*. Rick and I will be out just as soon as we can."

"But—"

"Crystal, *go*!"

The firmness of Kathy's voice forced the girl into action. Crystal ran to her mother and took her by the hand. When she snapped out of Kathy's magic, Lynn looked just as confused—and scared—as Crystal.

"What's going on? What happened?" Lynn wondered aloud.

"Go with Crystal," Kathy assured her. "It's okay. I'll take care of everything else. But go quickly. I don't know how much time we have."

Crystal led Lynn up the stairs by her hand.

With them safely out of the cellar, Kathy turned to Rick and touched his shoulder, which brought him out of the freeze.

"Hey, we have to go," Kathy told him.

He looked confused, but he adjusted faster than Crystal and Lynn had.

"Watch the bullet," Kathy warned him. She led him around the bullet, suspended in midair by her magic, and up the stairs.

The two of them had just made it out into the fresh air when they heard the bullet ricochet off the wall below, followed by the sound of Kurt crumpling to the ground.

"What was that?" Lynn asked.

"The bullet Rick fired," Kathy told her.

He looked at Kathy. "You think it worked?"

"Only one way to find out," she told him. "Want me to go?"

He shook his head. "I'll go. I have a couple more rounds. Just in case."

"Be careful," Kathy told him. When he disappeared down the stairs, she turned to Lynn. "Are you okay? Are you hurt?"

In the daylight, she saw just how worn the woman looked. There were red marks along her wrists where the rope had bound her. Worse, Kathy saw that Lynn's pants were torn and bloody.

Lynn clung to her daughter, ignoring her injuries. "I'll be okay. I'm just glad the nightmare is over."

"Well, not quite."

"We need to save Samantha," Crystal told her mother.

"Who's Samantha?" Lynn asked.

"My sister." Kathy tossed the answer over her shoulder when she noticed Rick coming back up the stairs. "So?"

Rick nodded. "He's dead."

Kathy let out the breath she didn't realize she'd been holding. "Okay. Now we need to go get my sister back."

CHAPTER 35

Rick walked into the driveway back at the main house with Kurt's body slung over his shoulders. Once he was in the middle of the open, he dropped the dead Fisher to the ground.

His body slumped down, and his lifeless form melded to the shape of the gravel. Blood continued to ooze out of the bullet hole in his chest, which had also transferred to Rick's back on the trip back to the house.

Bringing his hands up to cup his mouth, Rick shouted, "Come on out, you psychos! I brought home dinner!"

Pete and Donovan came out of the barn first. They kept their distance, especially as the door opened in the house and Jim and Sue walked out.

Upon seeing his deceased son, Jim turned to his wife. "Go back inside."

Her expression was hard to read. She didn't burst into tears and weep over the loss of her son, but she didn't seem indifferent either. Perhaps there was some scrap of maternal love in her, after all.

"Go back inside, Susan!" Jim ordered when his wife hadn't moved.

Glaring up at him, she turned back to the house and disappeared inside.

"Do you have a death wish?" Jim asked as he marched across the driveway toward Rick.

Pete and Donovan followed his lead and closed in on Rick as well.

Rick pulled out two smoke bombs from his pocket—more souvenirs found in the barn filled with stolen goods—and lit them with a lighter. He tossed them at the approaching Fishers.

The billowing smoke that ensued gave Kathy, Lynn, and Crystal the opportunity to dart to the back door of the house. They had been lying in wait in the woods. Rick had been the guinea pig.

Kathy wanted Lynn and Crystal to wait somewhere safe, but Lynn thought it was a bad idea for Kathy to go in the Fisher house alone and Crystal did not want to stay outside on her own again for fear of losing her mother.

So all three of them darted to the back door and slipped

inside, hoping that Sue Fisher would be too distracted from what was going on in the driveway to notice them, or that she would be easy to fend off.

The first thing Kathy noticed when she made it inside the house was that the whole place smelled almost like her house did every Thanksgiving. Delicious, savory scents filled the room from someone hard at work in the kitchen.

The several references the Fishers had made to eating up their victims suddenly appeared in Kathy's mind and her stomach turned at the smell she had once thought was delicious.

It would be a while before she could truly enjoy a Thanksgiving meal again.

The back door led into a mud room, or enclosed back patio. There was still the chill of outside, but the door into the house was open, letting the smells from the kitchen carry.

Kathy motioned for Lynn and Crystal to tuck against the wall while she peered into the kitchen to see just where Sue was.

She couldn't see around the corner, but she saw Samantha, tied up to a chair across the kitchen in the dining room.

Kathy looked back at Lynn and Crystal long enough to motion for them to stay where they were, then began to creep into the doorway, but stopped quick.

Sue was waiting for them, a grilling skewer brandished in her hand. "Get the hell out of my damn house, you miserable rodents!" She jabbed it toward Kathy for emphasis.

The witch was quick, kicking up her foot and knocking the skewer from the woman's hands. Then, back on both feet, Kathy pushed the woman hard so that she toppled on the ground.

Taking a cue from what she'd seen Rick do to Kurt earlier, Kathy jumped on the woman and pinned her down.

"Go!" she barked back at Lynn and Crystal.

The mother-daughter duo was already on the move, running by Kathy and Sue to get to Samantha.

Kathy was surprised by Sue's strength, who fought back hard, pushing against the witch and squirming under her hold to try to free herself. She managed to knock Kathy aside and get to her feet, but Kathy was on top of her once more, trying to knock her to the floor again to slow her down.

Her eyes scanned the kitchen island and the countertops. A pot of water was boiling on the stove and a cutting board with a knife and a half-chopped tomato sat beside it. Too far out of Kathy's reach. Not if she wanted to keep Sue back from getting to where Lynn and Crystal were trying to free Samantha.

As Kathy continued to push the woman over, Sue finally turned and pushed back. Kathy lost her footing and crashed hard into the corner of a cabinet that dug into her side and made the air rush out of her lungs. She banged against a decorative shelf hanging on the wall and sank down just before it came crashing down on top of her. Knickknacks and tchotchkes crashed to the floor, shattering and surrounding Kathy in several pieces of broken glass and ceramics.

"Kathy!" Crystal called out, then screamed when Sue turned on them.

"I'm going to slice you up, little girl," Sue threatened.

Lynn went into protector mode and grabbed the woman by the hair, pulling her away from her daughter. Sue thrashed about, trying to pull Lynn off of her.

The two struggled, banging into walls, knocking more decorations to the floor, all the while ping-ponging off the wall in the kitchen, where they bounced against the wooden island and the countertops.

Sue's hand went out for the knife on the cutting board. Lynn saw it, then dug her fingers tighter into the Fisher woman's hair.

"You little bitch," Sue grumbled. "My son should've shot you when he had the chance. After we kill you, I'll make sure to slice up your pretty little daughter and cook her up for dinner tonight."

In a flash of anger, Lynn shoved the woman's head down into the boiling water on the stove. As Sue thrashed, Lynn kept the woman's head submerged in the boiling water. Sue fought for her life as Lynn maintained her grip. Errant bursts of water spurted up around Sue's head and burned Lynn's hand, but she didn't stop. Not until several seconds later when Sue's body finally went limp.

Finally, she released her hold and jumped back as Sue's body fell to the floor bringing the boiling pot of water down with it. Lynn avoided looking at Sue's red, bloated, and blistered face.

She reached over and turned off the burner, then cradled her burned hand.

"That's one way to stop her," Kathy said from behind Lynn. With Crystal's help, she had already freed Samantha, who rubbed her wrists where the restraints had been.

"Is everyone okay?" Lynn asked.

Kathy nodded, then turned to Samantha and Crystal for confirmation.

Samantha smiled weakly. She had dried blood down the side of her face. "Better now. I'll be great just as soon as we get out of here."

"You're hurt, Mommy!" Crystal said.

The skin on Lynn's hand was red and angry, although not as bad as Sue's face was. She cast her hand to her side in a show of nonchalance. "I'll be fine."

"Okay, we need to go," Kathy said. She led them to the back door, but stopped when the remaining Fishers piled in from both the front and back doors at the same time.

They were surrounded.

CHAPTER 36

The four of them backed up slowly as Jim and his boys entered the house. None of the Fishers moved quickly, knowing that they had the girls trapped.

Jim gritted his teeth. "It's about damn time we settle this." He clenched his fists and took a step forward.

Crystal cowered behind her mother. Kathy clung to Samantha's arm that she had draped over her own shoulder for support. Slowly, the four of them backed away deeper into the short hallway that led to another part of the house.

"Dad…" Pete's voice was quiet, which seemed to grab Jim's attention among the tension.

Jim turned back and saw, before Pete could even tell him, his wife's body laying on the floor. Her face an angry red and covered in boils and sores from her terrible death. Her clothes were soaked from the deadly water. The pot lay on its side next to her.

When he turned back to the girls, there was venom in his eyes.

"Run!" Kathy pulled Samantha back, following Lynn and Crystal's lead into the closest room.

Jim and the other Fishers charged after them, but Lynn and Crystal managed to slam the door shut before they could get to it.

They had taken refuge in a front bedroom. Kathy slumped Samantha down on the bed, then rushed to the door to help hold it closed while Lynn and Crystal struggled to push a dresser in front of it.

With that secured, Kathy motioned to the bed, and the two women shoved the large bed frame up against the dresser barricading the door for additional protection.

Beneath the bed were boxes of storage, a whole litter of dust bunnies, and several cords tethered to the wall. So ordinary. So normal. Very much like Kathy's own bedroom. And yet this reality they were in was so out of her own world. Her version of *normal* had always been different from the rest of the world, but this was a whole new level of weird.

On the other side of the door, the Fishers pounded on the wood.

"You can't hide in there forever, you bitches!" Jim hollered.

"This is *our* house!" Pete added.

"Now what?" Crystal asked.

"Yeah, that door's not going to hold up forever," Lynn added.

Kathy nodded to the window.

"I'll skin you alive for this!" one of the Fishers shouted from the other side of the door.

"Why can't you freeze them?" Crystal asked.

"I can't do it through the door," Kathy said. "It doesn't work like that."

"Well, if we're going through the window, we need to do it before they realize we're escaping," Lynn said in a hushed tone.

Kathy nodded and then crossed to the window above the bedside table. It was small—it would definitely be a tight fit—but Kathy was sure all of them could make it out just fine. She made sure the lock was open, then braced against the window frame to try to open it.

It wouldn't budge.

The pounding on the other side of the door continued.

"What's the matter?" Samantha asked.

"It won't move," Kathy said. "I think it might be painted shut from the outside."

Crystal clung to her mother. "What are we going to do?"

Fists continued to beat on the other side of the door, along with curses and threats.

"Break it," Lynn said.

Kathy grabbed the lamp from the bedside table and used the decorative metal end of it to bash against the glass. She hit it once, twice, three times. Each time she hit it with more force, trying to smash the glass. It cracked, but wouldn't budge.

The poor diet over the last couple days was catching up to her, sapping her strength.

"Want me to try?" Samantha offered.

"No, I want you to rest," Kathy said. "We still have no idea what kind of long-term head injury you have." She dropped the lamp to the floor, then swiped off the rest of the contents of the table and climbed on. It wobbled under her feet.

Lynn rushed up to help steady it.

Kathy turned away from the window, wound up her foot, then delivered a backward kick into it. Again, she struck three times. Her body flailed and Crystal rushed up to hold her hands to steady her. On the third kick, her foot crashed through the window and she carefully retrieved it through the shattered glass falling from the frame.

"Give me the blanket."

Samantha stood and pulled the loose blanket from the bed.

Kathy took it and balled it around her fist to knock out as much of the glass from the frame as she could.

"Why did the pounding stop?" Crystal asked.

They had been so focused on the window that none of them had noticed.

"Do you think they know what we're doing?" Lynn whispered.

"We have to move faster," Samantha told her sister.

With the glass knocked out, Kathy opened the blanket and lay it over the edge of the broken window. "Lynn, you go first."

Crystal burst into tears and reached for her mom. "No! I don't want you to go."

"You'll go next," Kathy assured her. "But we can only go one at a time and your mom should go first so she can catch you." She wondered if Lynn's frail body would have the strength to catch her daughter after the week of torment from Kurt, but they were all running on adrenaline now, so Kathy knew Lynn was going to do what needed to be done for her daughter.

Lynn climbed up on the bedside table and leaned against the frame to put her feet through first. Then, just like going down a water slide, she slipped out of sight.

Kathy stuck her head through the window and saw Lynn had fallen into an overgrown bush under the window. She stood and then gave a thumbs-up. "Okay, Crystal, you next."

The witches helped the little girl up onto the table and then through the window.

"You should go first," Samantha told Kathy once Crystal and Lynn were safely out the window.

Kathy shook her head. "No. I need to be here in case—"

There was noise on the other side of the door again. Not fists this time, but something heavier.

Then the door splintered open as the business end of an ax broke through the wood.

"Okay! I'm going." Samantha didn't waste anymore time arguing. She turned and launched herself out the window.

Kathy jumped back up on the table to climb out herself.

Donovan's head appeared in the hole in the door. "They're escaping! Out through the window! Get outside!"

Jumping through the window, Kathy landed hard in the bush and was surprised to see that she was alone. She took a quick survey of her surroundings and saw Samantha, Lynn, and Crystal all rushing toward the barn across the driveway.

Gunshots hit the barn, signaling that the Fishers were outside.

Kathy ran around the side of the house, taking the remaining Fishers by surprise. They all stood on the porch. She put up her hands and froze them, then ran across the driveway to join the rest of her ragtag group.

"You all okay?" Rick's eyes scanned over each of them.

Kathy nodded. "We're fine. Now light it up."

He smirked. "Don't mind if I do." He ran across the driveway, keeping a weary eye on the frozen Fishers.

"What's he going to do?" Crystal asked.

Kathy nodded around the back of the barn. "We should go over there and take cover. And Crystal, make sure to cover your ears really good. This is going to hurt."

Rick ran back, breathless and smiling. "The fuse is lit.

Should be anytime now and the whole thing will go—"

He was cut off by the largest explosion that the witches had ever heard in their lives. The force knocked them all to the ground. Immediately, Kathy's ears began to ring. She could *see* Crystal screaming, but she couldn't hear her. Not at first.

Slowly, they got up and Kathy motioned for Samantha to stay with Lynn and Crystal under the cover of the barn, while she and Rick ventured out to inspect the house.

When she came around the corner, the large black flames billowing from the remnants of the house is what hit Kathy first. Then the heat licking her face. And then she noticed pieces of the house scattered around the driveway, including the dead bodies of the Fishers.

It was over. They were free.

CHAPTER 37

As the flames consumed what was left of the Fisher house, Kathy stood at the edge of the driveway beside the barn and looked around.

"They're gone," Rick said from beside her. His voice was distant. Muffled. The effects of the blast still ringing in Kathy's ears.

"I'm looking for bodies." Her own voice sounded funny. She was hearing it clearer inside her head than out. "I need to know that they're dead. That this is really over."

Rick was quiet and helped her look. He pointed toward the barn, where Kurt's body lay against the weathered wood.

Kathy nodded, then scanned the rest of the debris. Jim and Pete lay next to each other, buried under a pile of rubble. By the amount of blood pouring from their bodies, Kathy knew that they were dead, too.

"Where's Donovan?" she muttered. Her eyes struggled to stay open against the heat of the flames, even from a safe distance away.

Once again, Rick pointed to a spot. Kathy squinted and saw Donovan's head laying several feet away from his limp body.

"Oh." She brought a hand to her mouth, overcome with emotion. Several days ago, she had never met these people. Now she was glad that they were dead. She had never felt this relief at someone's death before. It made her feel a change in her soul. How was she any better than the Fishers?

"They're all gone. The madness can end." Rick rubbed Kathy's arms as he stood behind her and tried to pull her back away from the fire, but she held her ground.

"I don't know."

"What do you mean?"

Her shoulders sagged and she turned to face Rick. "We just blew up their house. We killed all of them."

"Kathy, they tried to kill *us*," he reminded her. "They tortured me, Crystal's mom, probably even Clay and Larry."

She nodded. "I know. And I know they don't deserve my sympathy. It's just…it doesn't feel right." She gestured to the flames. "This feels…too much. As horrible as they were, they were people. My job as a witch—my *instinct*—is to protect people. This makes me feel like I'm a murderer. That I'm no better than them."

"But you *did* protect people, Kathy. You protected me, your sister, Crystal, and her mom. You saved us with your powers. The Fishers, they were bad people. If you hadn't helped me stop them—kill them—then they would try to hurt us again. We were just protecting ourselves."

She shrugged. "A court is going to have a hard time believing that with the extent that we went to."

"But a good lawyer will point out that we only used the resources that we had—the ones we got from the Fishers themselves."

Kathy didn't have anything to say to that. They both fell into silence. Finally, Rick looked at the barn they were standing next to. He set his hand on the weathered wood.

"This barn is our evidence. So is the souvenir barn buried in the woods."

She scrunched her brow in confusion.

"They sliced me up in this barn. My blood will still be all over their knives. Clay is…Clay died in the souvenir barn. Not to mention all that stuff that they stole from their other victims before us. All of it is more than enough evidence to point the finger at the Fishers and prove that this—" He waved to the burning house again. "—was in self-defense."

Kathy didn't have time to offer her response. Samantha limped over, using the wall of the barn for support. When she got closer to them, Kathy stepped toward her and offered her arm to help.

As the sisters clung together to hold each other up, Rick asked, "How are you doing? I saw you take a nasty hit to the head."

Samantha nodded ever so slightly. "I've been better. But I think the bleeding has stopped. At least on the outside. Hopefully there's none on the inside. And my vision is much clearer now. I think I just have a bad concussion."

"You'll probably have to take it easy for the next couple weeks," Kathy said. "I can help when we get home."

Samantha smirked. "Home. That sounds great right about now. I'll be okay." She pointed to her car buried in the weeds. "Do you think you can fix it up so we can get out of here? The Fishers did something so it wouldn't start when they chased us out of the cabin."

Rick nodded. "I'll take a look at it. Hopefully Crystal's mom's is around here too."

"Lynn," Kathy said. "Her name is Lynn."

They looked back down to the back of the barn where they had all taken cover from the blast. Lynn sat on the ground, rocking Crystal in her lap as if she were a baby. Even though she was eight years old, Crystal had been through so much that she deserved to be coddled. In her mother's arms, she was in a deep sleep.

Good, Kathy thought. *Hopefully she can move past this*

without too many nightmares.

Samantha's voice pulled Kathy back to their little trio. "So it's actually over?"

"It is," Rick said.

"I wish we could've saved Larry," Samantha said. She looked to Rick. "And Clay."

He nodded. "Me too. But their sacrifices helped the rest of us survive." He turned to Kathy. "You helped me see that."

She smiled and looked down.

Samantha looked between the two of them. "Maybe it's the crack in my head or the lack of a proper meal in the last couple days, but I'm not following."

"When Clay was captured, it gave me time to escape and get far enough away from the Fishers so that they couldn't find me," Rick started.

"And because Rick had survived, he saved *us* from the Fishers when they chased *you and me* out," Kathy added.

"And since you were saved, then that allowed you to save Crystal, whose father had sacrificed himself so that she and her mother—Lynn—were safe."

"I wouldn't say that Lynn was exactly *safe*, but she survived," Samantha said. Her eyes wandered back to Lynn and Crystal, who were still curled in on each other.

"But Crystal has her mother back," Kathy said. "And that's what matters."

"None of this will bring my friend back—or Crystal's dad—

but saving the rest of us is a good legacy for Clay and Larry to have," Rick said. "Even if they never met each other."

"Funny how things like that effect us," Samantha said. She took a deep breath, then changed the subject. "Well, if you think you can fix my car, then I better go break the good news and break up their reunion. I'm ready to go home. I need to see Josh." Then, as an afterthought, "And Steven."

Kathy chuckled. "Me too. I guess you were right."

"About what?" Samantha asked.

"This trip was a terrible idea."

Samantha raised her eyebrows. "And I'll be saying 'I told you so' for the rest of our lives. But you were right about one thing: we did get closer."

"Well, at least there's a bright side." Kathy laughed. She felt lighter than she had in days. Now that the worst of the tragedy was behind them, she realized that all of her worries before this had paled in comparison.

"I'll get started on the cars," Rick said, "just as soon as the fire burns down a little. I don't want anything to spark that big flame and risk our lives after we survived all of that."

"Good thinking," Samantha said, then started off back toward Lynn and Crystal.

When she was gone and out of earshot—which wasn't very far with their ears still ringing from the blast—Kathy looked up at Rick.

"I still don't like the idea of you taking the fall for all of this."

"I really don't think there will be a fall," he said. "I did what I needed to protect myself. I believe a jury will see it that way."

"And what if they don't?"

He shrugged, then winced from the cuts Pete had slashed into him. "If they don't see it that way, then…then I guess I'll be the only one of us who gets a life sentence for murder. One is better than five. Especially when the rest of you have a family to return to."

Kathy shook her head. "I can't let you do that."

He took her hands in his and stared right into her eyes. "You saved my life, and gave Clay's death a better purpose. Covering for you and your sister, that's the least I can do as payment."

"But I'm not asking for a payment."

"No, but I'm doing this for you anyway."

They held each other's stare, sizing the other up. Something deeper burned within both of them. Something they hadn't been able to address until now.

Kathy leaned up on her toes and brought her lips to his. It felt perfect. She felt safe. Even though she knew that she would never truly get to know him. That the two of them would never have a future together. That this would be the only kiss they ever shared.

When she pulled away, both of them smiled at one another.

"That was…nice," he said with a grin. "Been wanting to do that for a while now."

"Me too, but dodging attacks from psychopaths doesn't

really warrant a romantic evening vibe."

Their laughter faded. Kathy chanced a look back at Samantha, who turned away when she saw Kathy notice her looking.

"Thank you for all that you've done for us," Kathy told him. "For me. I'll never forget it."

"And thank you."

She reached up and touched his cheek, tempted to kiss him again. "I'll never forget you."

Everything happens for a reason.

The Fates pay Samantha and Kathy a visit when the sisters' misstep, which left a man the target of a vampire bite, leads to unimaginable consequences in the future.

Unconvinced of the effects of one bite, the sisters travel forward to the future, where, at first, everything seems perfectly normal…until nightfall when the world seems to plunge into dystopia.

Soon, the sisters find themselves on the run from a vampiric empire taking over the city, and possibly even the country, as they uncover terrible truths about their future. With their efforts to return to their time having failed, the sisters fear that they may be stuck in the horrific future that they've inadvertently created.

The Fates is the fourteenth and final book in the Coven series, which is part of the Art of Magic universe, containing the Lost By Magic and the Under the Moon series.

THE FATES

COVEN: BOOK 14

Read on for an excerpt of the final book in the Coven series!

DAVID NETH

CHAPTER 1

- JANUARY 1991 -

Samantha and Kathy sprinted through the night. The winter wind whipped around them, but they paid it no mind. They charged on over the city roads covered with slush from the previous day's snow.

The trouble was, they didn't know where exactly they were running to. Kathy's power had recently grown. Now, instead of her time specialty allowing her to only momentarily freeze people in time, her powers allowed her to witness moments in a future time, right in her mind. Premonitions. Psychic visions. Whatever it was called, she could, in a sense, see the future.

And what she saw terrified her.

"What did it look like in the vision?" Samantha's head was craned to the left as she looked down driveways along W 21st

Street. Kathy, meanwhile, inspected the houses to the right.

"It was just a skinny driveway," Kathy said. "A garage at the back of it. A small yard beside it. Just like all of these—"

A man's screams cut her off. Somewhere down toward the end of the block. Near Chestnut Street.

The girls sped up to reach it faster, but the cries died off.

"Where did it come from?" Kathy stopped and looked around.

"This way." Samantha led her sister to a house that seemed to be very well-kept. The biggest flaws were some worn siding and cracked sidewalks in front. Even the car parked in the driveway looked to be newer. Maybe an '88 or '89.

At the back of the driveway, though, they saw two men who appeared to be kissing. Upon closer inspection, they saw that they weren't actually kissing. Instead, the one man was biting the other.

"A vampire?" Samantha asked.

"Just like I saw." Kathy raced up. "Hey! Leave him alone!"

The man who had been bitten fell to the ground. His neck dripped with blood. The skin around it looked inflamed and angry.

Not half as angry as the other man, who remained standing. The one whose face looked as white as a ghost and who had blood dripping around his mouth. The one who wore sharp clothing, all in black. An odd sight for the setting.

"No!" Samantha called. "You killed him!"

"I improved him," the pale man said. "Perhaps you'd like to be next?" He lunged at them and the sisters jumped back. He laughed at their fear.

Kathy pulled a wooden stake from her jacket pocket and passed it to Samantha. "Here! I pulled it from the garage before we left."

The older sister grumbled as she took the small weapon. Her eyes remained on the vampire in front of them. She had never battled with one before and she didn't like the idea of having to get so close to him in order to stop him.

Kathy pulled a second stake from her pocket and the sisters spread out, splitting the vampire's focus.

As the three of them squared off, the vampire took several lunges at the witches to scare them, but never made contact. Kathy knew that if he wanted to, he could strike them down faster than either of them could. What they needed was a distraction. A way to split the vampire's focus even further. Like—

"Kathy! The car!" Samantha noticed that the car in the driveway had a combination lock on the door handle. Something equipped with that level of safety likely had an alarm as well.

Kathy looked to her sister, then down to the car. In one quick jab, she slammed the tip of the stake into the hood of the car. Instantly, the alarm sounded and the headlights began flashing.

The vampire shielded his eyes as the lights on the car began to flash. Meanwhile, behind him, his latest victim began to rise to his feet. His skin had turned a ghostly shade of white, just like his attacker's. What was more, the bite mark on his neck had faded completely, leaving only dried blood in its place.

"Uh…" Samantha hesitated as she suddenly realized that there were *two* vampires to contend with now.

The first vampire stepped back next to the second and smirked at the witches. "You're too late. He's now officially one of us. You're too late."

Kathy put up her hands to freeze them, but the first vampire hissed at them and she jumped. When she turned to try again, they were gone.

"Well, that was unexpected," Samantha said.

"And unfortunate," Kathy said. "We lost an innocent man and created a monster."

Samantha looked around. "Yeah, and we need to get out of here before one of the neighbors calls the cops about the noise from this car and then *we're* being investigated for his disappearance."

While neither of them liked the fact that they had lost someone they were meant to protect, their only choice left was to protect themselves. So off they ran.

CHAPTER 2

"I promised you I'd make it up to you." Samantha presented her husband with a cup of coffee as he sat in the living room.

Josh was tucked in close next to his dad, his eyes glued on the TV.

Steven laughed and reached for the cup. "Not quite the romantic evening I was expecting, but I guess I'll take it."

Their two-year anniversary dinner had been interrupted by the urgency of Kathy's vision the night before. And the fact that they hadn't even been able to save the man was just more salt in the wound.

"Honey, it's okay." He set the mug down on the end table, then reached for his his wife's hand and pulled her into his lap.

"Mom, go 'way!"

"That's not nice," Steven scolded in a soft tone. "We don't say that."

Josh had already moved on, reverting to his zombie-like state as he watched the cartoons dance across the television screen.

Samantha didn't like how much they let Josh watch TV, but sometimes it was the only way to get things done around the house. And other than in the mornings on the weekends and every evening, he didn't watch nearly as much as some other kids. Then again, what Kathy let him do while they were at work was out of Samantha's control.

"I was a little annoyed last night, yes," Steven went on.

She scoffed. "More than a little…"

"But I got over it," he said. "After I put Josh to bed, it was nice to have the house to myself for a change. I got to watch a little TV of my own. Have my own snack."

She raised her eyebrows. "So you're saying you don't want a makeup for last night?"

He smirked. "I didn't say *that*. In fact, I think you owe me."

Samantha feigned ignorance. "Doesn't the coffee cover it?"

"Oh, not even close!"

She laughed and leaned in to kiss him.

"Have your sister watch Josh tonight," he said. "We can book a hotel room."

Another burst of laughter. "Okay. Let's not get wild here."

He pulled her even closer. Not that there was any way that was possible. She was already sitting in his lap. "I just want to be alone with you."

"And I want the same thing," she said. "And we will. Tonight. We'll go to dinner, then come back here after Josh has gone to bed. Maybe Kathy will be cozy down here in the living room so you and I can get cozy upstairs—"

She stopped and pulled away from her husband. "Steven?"

He wasn't moving. Wasn't reacting to anything she was saying, like he had been moments before.

Then she realized that the TV wasn't playing anything anymore either. She craned around and saw that it was frozen.

"Kathy!" she called up the stairs. Samantha tried to extract herself from her husband's grip, which had been a loving embrace only moments ago but now felt like a prison. "Kathy! Did you freeze us?"

Seconds later, her younger sister raced down the stairs. "Sam! What's going on? Everything outside has stopped! I was watching the snow fall and then—hey, what happened to Steven?" Kathy scrunched her eyebrows together when she saw that he was sitting with his arms in the same position they had been when they were wrapped around his wife.

"You mean *you* didn't do this?"

"My power has grown, sure, but not that much!" Kathy said. "I was actually just upstairs reading about premonitions and I think my power is growing in a whole different way than all of this."

"Then who did this?" Samantha was equally confused as her sister.

"Well, I'll tell you, Clo, I could see that coming a mile away!" an old woman said from the dining room. "He's had his eye on her since they were kids!"

"But she loved Greg," another lady's voice said. "They were engaged! I thought the two of them had what it takes!"

A third lady scoffed. "Oh, please, Atro. Nothing beats out your first true love. Nobody else compares!"

The sisters eyed each other, then stepped around the corner into the dining room. Three old women sat at the end of the table. Each of them had knitting needles in their hands, working away at different parts of the large tapestry that lay across the dining room table, extending off the end of it and spilling onto the floor on the opposite side. The tapestry had a unique and beautiful design, although there were many imperfections. Knots and lines out of place from the patterns, even though the whole of it still was something to marvel.

"Excuse me?" Samantha asked, suddenly feeling as though she needed to be polite even though these women had invaded *her* house. "Who are you?"

The woman sitting in the middle turned around and looked at them, then held her hand to her chest as she laughed. "Oh! Honey, you scared me!"

"You have to be careful, Clo, or we'd have to find someone else to finish up Taylor Miller's stitch work," the woman to her left said.

"We might as well," the third one said. "Look how she's gone and messed it all up. Clo, that stitching is horrendous!"

"Me? It's not *my* fault!"

Kathy cleared her throat. "Who the hell are you people?"

"Oh, my apologies!" the lady on the left said. "My name is Lachesis, but the girls here call me Lakie for short. Then there's Clotho, or Clo, and over there is Atropos, but we just call her Atro." She indicated with a head nod who she was talking about.

"Why are you here?" Samantha asked.

"Well, we're the Fates," Lakie said.

"We typically don't allow ourselves to be seen," Atro cut in, all the while keeping her eyes on her stitching.

"But we thought this was especially necessary," Clo added.

"You see," Lakie picked up, "you've failed in your duties as witches."

Kathy raised her eyebrows. "Excuse me?"

"Is this about last night?" Samantha asked. "We did the best we could!"

"Ah!" Atro raised a finger, then resumed her needlework. "But your best was not enough."

"You can't blame us for that!" Samantha said. "We tried. We failed. Evil spread. Someone's life is essentially over. Don't you think we already feel terrible about all of that?"

"We can't save *every* person," Kathy added. "As hard as we try to."

"But you see, from that terrible *mistake*, you have significantly altered the course of time," Clo said.

"Altered the fates of so many others," Lakie said.

Samantha tucked her hair behind her ears, then put her hands on her hips. "What are you talking about? Nobody else was there last night."

"We're not talking about the past," Atro said. "We're talking about the future."

"We're not responsible for the future!" Kathy blurted.

"Ah, but in fact, you are." Clo waved her needle in the direction of the witches. "With every life you save, you preserve the future. And with every life lost…"

"Just take a look at the tapestry." Lakie pointed out the line of stitching she was working on. Although the sisters knew nothing about how knitting and crocheting worked, they both could see that the line of stitching had gone severely off-course from the rest of the design.

"Oh, yes, that's terrible, Lakie," Atro said.

She shrugged. "It was the best I could do with what I was given!"

"Will someone explain to us what's going on?" Samantha demanded.

"In terms that we can understand," Kathy added.

"This is the tapestry of time," Atro explained.

"Collectively, as the Fates, we stitch it together based on the actions of those in the world," Lakie added.

"Each person's actions affect someone else's life in one or another," Clo said. "Like our lives, the tapestry is tightly woven together."

"But it's not without mistakes," Lakie said.

"Look at this line here." Clo pointed to a knot in the tapestry. "This was the moment you two failed to save Stockley from Aldric's bite."

"Stockley? Aldric?" Kathy asked. "Were those the names of the men last night?"

"The *vampires*," Lakie corrected.

"The undead," Clo added.

"The ones who wish to defy the work we do," Atro finished.

"In the future, those two vampires have gone on to gain too much power," Lakie said.

"Witches, wizards, and even good-hearted vampires cannot stop them," Clo said.

"And the rest of humanity has had to suffer from their reign," Atro said.

"In the future, we, as the Fates, have no influence over anyone's choices," Lakie explained. "The vampires are in *complete* control."

"And that will lead to the end of our tapestry," Clo explained. "Something we've been creating since the dawn of humanity."

Kathy crossed her arms, feeling the guilt of their misstep hit her hard. "So you came here just to tell us we screwed up and that, because of us, humanity is going to die?"

All three women looked at each other, then burst out laughing.

"No!" Clo blurted.

"You two don't wield that kind of power!" Lakie said, still chuckling.

"We came here to ask for your help!" Atro clarified.

"And you thought you'd start off by insulting us?" Kathy asked.

Lakie rolled her eyes and shook her head. "Oh, please! The *dramatics* of these witches! No, we were simply alerting you to the problem!"

"And so what kind of help were you hoping to get out of us?" Samantha asked.

"We want to offer something we've never done before," Atro said.

"We will unravel part of our tapestry so that the two of you can unknot out tapestry and restore order," Lakie explained.

"In a sense, we will be turning back time to allow you to fix what you failed to do before," Clo said.

There was a significant silence that followed the Fates' proposition. Samantha and Kathy both turned to each other. Even without Samantha's telepathic abilities, they knew what the other was thinking.

"And you expect us to agree to that?" Samantha asked.

"You have to!" Atro said, all laughter from her face gone.

"We don't *have to* do anything," Kathy said. "Look, we're sorry that you're disappointed in us—we're also sorry we weren't able to save that man last night—but *you* try doing our job for a day and see if you have a perfect streak!"

"And we're not going to risk going back in time," Samantha said. "There are too many variables. Even with your foresight as the Fates."

"Yeah, how do we know that you even have that kind of power?" Kathy added. "How do we know you're not going to slip up and send us back fifteen years and we'll have to relive a chunk of our lives and hope that everything turns out the same?"

"That's a lot of trust you're asking of us, all for one single vampire that we let be created."

Lakie rose from her seat. "A vampire that will help lead to the end of humanity as we know it! A vampire that will help turn all of civilization into mindless vampiric *zombies* if they don't follow willingly."

"These vampires will be out of our control!" Atro said. "Without you correcting your mistake, we have no ability to influence how these circumstances will play out."

"Sounds like a problem for you," Kathy said. "Not us."

"Wait." Clo remained calm. Her knitting needles no longer moving. "I have a proposition for you girls, seeing as though you have your…hesitations."

Samantha put her hands on her hips. "And that would be…?"

"What if we sent you *forward* in time, so you can witness the destruction yourselves?"

The two other Fates gasped.

"But that would require starting a new tapestry from scratch!" Lakie said.

"We've never done that before!" Atro added.

"For this, I'm willing to take the time," Clo said. "And with the present paused—and possibly remade—it's work we'd have to do anyway." Her eyes darted to the sisters. "You'd be able to see firsthand how bad this world is that we're trying to avoid. That way, you'll have no choice but to agree to help us stop it."

Samantha and Kathy both studied her, intrigued by the proposition, but fearful for what it might entail.

"So…what do you say?" Clo asked.

"Can we talk about this privately?" Kathy asked.

"Go ahead." Clo gestured for them to go.

Samantha and Kathy stepped into the living room, where Steven and Josh were still frozen on the couch. Moments later, they heard the giggling and cackling of laughter from the Fates as they resumed their gossip.

"I'm not sure about this," Samantha said in a hushed tone to her sister. "It seems too risky."

Kathy shrugged. "I don't know. I think it might be kind of

fun to see our future selves. I mean, when are we ever going to get the chance to again?"

"But what if we can't get back?"

"The Fates are sending us, I don't think we'll have a problem getting back. Besides, it's the future, not the past. So we won't even need to be careful about changing anything because when we come back to the present, everything we do in the future will be reset."

"Will it, though?" Samantha gestured toward the dining room. "With the Fates out there, everything is pre-destined, isn't it?"

Kathy shook her head. "No, they said it doesn't work like that. We still have free will. The future is made up of limitless possibilities. Fate only outlines those possibilities based on our choices made by our free will."

Samantha crossed her arms and looked at her sister. "When did you become an expert on this?"

"About five minutes ago when they explained how it works." She eyed her sister. "You don't think we can trust them."

"I didn't say that."

"But it's true."

"Okay." Samantha shrugged. "So I'm not sure we should. Is that so bad?"

"No. It's natural to be cautious—especially with our history. But they're the *Fates*, Sam! If we can't trust them, who can we trust? Besides, nothing ever happens in life without a little trust."

Samantha rolled her eyes. "All right, enough with the pop psychology tidbits. I'm just not sure I want to see that future they're talking about if it's so bad."

"So then we let them send us back in time to yesterday, and we can stop the vampires and avoid all of this."

Samantha breathed out a sigh, still unsure. "I just...I don't know how one simple vampire could be so dire."

Kathy looked down at her nails. "Well, the only way we're going to know that is by having the Fates send us into the future. And we can have some fun with it, too. See Josh all grown up—and the new baby."

Samantha's hand went to her belly. Her second pregnancy hadn't started showing yet, but the signs were there. Hormonal shifts. Cravings. Other changes to her body.

What a gift it would be to glimpse her children in the future. Nobody, as far as she knew, had ever had the chance before.

"Okay, think of it this way," Kathy went on. "Even if it turns out that we *can't* trust the Fates and we're suddenly stuck in this terrible future, all we need to do is track down your kids and our future selves and have them help us get back to this time. After all, each generation of magic is stronger than the next. Hopefully time travel is right on the cusp of magic."

Samantha sighed and nodded. "I mean, that does alleviate my fears a little bit."

"Then let's go give them our answer." Kathy led them back to the living room, where the three Fates were working away, giggling and joking and talking as if they hadn't just given the sisters such a monumental offer.

"So?" Clo asked. "What have you decided?"

"We'll take your offer to glimpse the future," Kathy said.

Atro smiled. "We knew you'd make the right choice."

"Just one question," Samantha cut in.

"Of course!" Clo said cheerfully.

"This won't affect our present lives at all?"

Atro shook her head. "Not at all. You will be traveling to a version of the future that we predict based on your current actions. Whatever happens in the future stays in the future."

"Almost like Vegas," Lakie said with a giggle. "So, are you ready?"

"Now?" Samantha blurted. "We're going *now*? Don't we get to say goodbye to our family?"

"Why?" Clo asked. "Sure, *you* will be leaving for a while, but when you come back you'll come right back to this moment. Steven and Josh—and the rest of the world, for that matter—will be unaware that time had frozen at all."

"We'll simply hit pause on reality and are going to pluck you into a different one for a little while before dropping you back in this one and letting it play again," Atro explained.

Kathy looked over and saw that her sister was starting to get cold feet, so she plunged on with what they had already decided.

"Okay. So what do we need to..."

Her words trailed off as an intense light came over them. And then they were gone.

CHAPTER 3

". . . Do?" Kathy finished slowly as the wave of light passed. She looked around the house—her house—and didn't initially notice anything different.

But after a few seconds, all the differences started rolling in, coming at her like sensory overload.

First off, the Fates were no longer sitting at the dining room table.

Second, the temperature was now much warmer—almost sticky. One quick glance outside told her that it was now summer time. A far cry from the wintry mid-January conditions that they were in moments before.

She picked up on little things next. For one, the flowers on the dining room table were different. The pictures on the walls, many of which of people she didn't quite recognize. Even the rug underneath the dining room table wasn't the same as it had been in Kathy's time.

"Are you okay?" Samantha asked, breaking into Kathy's thoughts.

"Yeah. Just taking it all in."

"I know. It's weird. It's the same but…not." Samantha stepped into the living room, which was empty of people.

"What is it?" Kathy joined her and noticed that the furniture had changed, as did the books on the shelves.

"Steven and Josh are gone."

"Well, yeah. It's the future."

"But then…where are they? Where am I? My future self, that is. Or did we take the place of our future selves?"

Kathy stepped toward the front door and glanced in the mirror that hung beside the coat rack. Glad to know at least some things were the same. Like, for instance, her face.

"Well, I don't look any older," she said. "So unless I've aged *incredibly* well, I think it's safe to say that we're still us. So our future selves are around here somewhere."

"I wish we knew how far into the future we went," Samantha murmured as her eyes roamed over the house. "What year is it? That would help us figure out where our future selves might—"

"Who are you?"

Both sisters turned to see a woman in the dining room. She

was young, looked to be about their age, with long black hair that was pulled back away from her face. She wore cutoff jeans and a yellow shirt.

Kathy looked to Samantha, then back at the woman. "Uh…who are *you*?"

The woman's face furrowed. "Kathy?"

Do you know her? Samantha pinged in Kathy's mind.

Not that I can remember, Kathy thought back. *Try searching her mind for any memories that would help us figure out who she is.*

Kathy could tell Samantha was quietly focusing her power in the woman's direction. And then the woman seemed to recognize Samantha's probe.

She charged at the sisters and knocked Samantha to the ground. Kathy stepped out of the way and raised her hands to freeze the woman, but she wouldn't freeze.

As if recognizing the attempt at magic, the woman turned to the door, raised her own hands, and the two front doors swung open on their own. Then, with another flick of her hands, Samantha and Kathy both scooted across the hardwood floor toward the threshold.

"Get out of here," the woman said. "And don't come back."

Samantha and Kathy wasted no time getting to their feet and running out into the hot summer sun. Behind them, the doors to their own house slammed shut.

THANK YOU

This project would not have been possible without the support of my Kickstarter backers! Thank you all for your support!

Samantha Newberry
Sarah B.
Leslie Twitchell
Marlene Renteria
Rowan Stone
John Idlor
Erik S
Dead Fish Books
Troy Hill
Lou Paduano
Alexandra Corrsin
Daniel.D
Gary Phillips
Deborah Hedges

Thank you to the DN Publishing VIP Club members over at Patreon! Become a member and enjoy weekly perks!

Tracy O'Neil
Marguerite Goosby

patreon.com/DNPublishing

FIND ALL THE BOOKS IN THE COVEN SERIES!

More by the Author

To find more books by the author, visit
DavidNethBooks.com/Books

* * *

Subscribe to his newsletter to be the first to know of new releases and special deals!
DavidNethBooks.com/Newsletter

* * *

If you enjoyed the book, please consider leaving a review on Goodreads or the retailer you bought it from. Reviews help potential readers determine whether they'll enjoy a book, so any comments on what you thought of the story would be very helpful!

About the Author

David Neth is the author of the Coven series, the Under the Moon series, Heat series, the Fuse series, and other stories. He lives in Batavia, NY, where he dreams of a successful publishing career and opening his own bookstore.

Also writes small town romance as D. Allen.

www.DavidNethBooks.com

www.facebook.com/DavidNethBooks

www.ingramcontent.com/pod-product-compliance
Lightning Source LLC
Chambersburg PA
CBHW020752310726
48969CB00002B/507
9781963602272